THE
BRIDGE
AT
DAWN

A NOVEL

KRIN VAN TATENHOVE

THE
BRIDGE
AT
DAWN

A NOVEL

KRIN VAN TATENHOVE

Cover image: Krin Van Tatenhove via Midjourney

Cover design and interior formatting provided by Casselberry Creative Design.

Story Sanctum Publishing
Bloomingdale, IL

ISBN: 979-8-9886653-8-0

Dedicated to Pieter Van Tatenhove
Firstborn, fellow writer, gentle soul
I love you with all my heart

And to every person currently living on the street

What mystery breaks over me now?
In its shadow I come into life.
- Rainer Maria Rilke, from *The Book of Hours*

I believe there's a ghost of a chance
We can find someone to love...
- Neil Peart

Table of Contents

Prologue

Summer 2023

San Francisco's summer fog engulfed the Golden Gate Bridge. It was near dawn, the appointed time, and already the mist was lightening from gray to a softer shade of white. Henry could hear early morning commuters streaming into the city on the opposite side, cloaked in gloom, their whooshing tires masking the roar of ocean breakers. Droplets of moisture clung to his dark hair and eyebrows.

As he walked along the bayside railing, he wondered if Cindy would be here. He recalled the warning he had received from Jean, and he shook his head. He was so far out of his comfort zone—led by his heart, not logic—that he barely recognized himself, a reminder that recent events had forever changed the course of his life.

He squinted through the dampness, rubbing his eyes, the density of the fog allowing only a few yards of visibility. He had been confident about his decision, but now he was beginning to feel foolish, even duped.

Suddenly, a figure materialized in front of him. A few steps further and he could see that it was her.

Her damp clothes clung to her skin, and she looked at him with those intense hazel eyes that always been so hard to read. She wiped a wet strand of hair from her forehead.

"I didn't know if you would come," she said.

"It seemed like the necessary thing to do," he said. "For both of us."

She nodded, gripped the railing, and began to lean her tall, athletic body forward, lifting both her feet off the bridge's sidewalk. He reached for her in a panic, his heart skipping a beat, and in that instant the fog cleared enough to glimpse the icy waters of the Pacific far below.

1

Early Spring 2023

Henry opened his eyes, unzipped his tent flap, then crawled out to stand in the sunrise that slanted beneath the overpass. Humidity clung to his skin like wet cotton. From the distance, approaching quickly and swelling with immediacy, came the wail of an emergency vehicle.

Why do they call them sirens? he thought, shaking off the night. *These aren't mythological vixens luring us to our doom. Just sharp reminders that tragedy is with us at all hours and all places. The whisper of death touches every cheek. Do not ask for whom the siren sounds. It sounds for thee.*

He smiled grimly, took a breath of dank air, and surveyed the makeshift encampment around him: tarps and boxes, worn and tattered tents, some of them rustling as people stirred from their sleep. Mumbling voices rose against the hiss of traffic from above. A man in a ragged army jacket fed newspaper into a barrel fire, despite the risk of drawing attention from the authorities. The city, long known for its tolerance of the homeless, seemed to have reached its limit, pressured by citizens from adjoining neighborhoods. Just a week earlier, heavy-handed police officers had dispersed a similar camp. Everyone was on edge.

Henry's neighbors called this Freedom Camp, a name he thought was both hopeful and ironic. He had heard so many of their stories. Soaring prices for food, medicine, and childcare demanded a juggling act that some couldn't manage, especially on minimum wages. Affordable housing, debated by armchair politicians, rarely became a reality. Most of all, there was the toll of mental illness and addiction that led to downward mobility. The numbers of those experiencing homelessness, rising even before COVID-19, were still outpacing services after the pandemic. These citizens knew the underbelly of the American Dream, not just its advertised freedoms.

A man with tangled dreadlocks approached, pushing a shopping cart filled with an odd mix of junk, including broken pieces of plastic dolls, their faces peering out though the metal grid. When he came near, he looked at Henry with dark, penetrating eyes.

"Do I know you from another life?" he asked.

"I've lived a lot of them," said Henry, "so it gets a bit hazy. But I think I'd remember you."

The man grinned. "Do you have a cigarette, brother?"

"Don't smoke," said Henry, his eyes straying to the man's black T-shirt. Emblazoned on it in white were the words *Got Hope?* He smiled, which made the man look down at his own chest.

"That's the message, bro. Light up the darkness, yeah? Go full-blown into the battle!"

The man startled cackling, then turned his back and shuffled further into the encampment.

Henry watched him recede. He didn't romanticize those living on the streets. He had witnessed predatory drug traffickers, the poison of meth and opioids bought and sold. He knew the dangers of criminals hiding in their midst, scavenging last scraps from the vulnerable. He knew that unmedicated mental illness could quickly erupt into violence. He lamented the sheer amount of trash scattered by these residents, a blight on urban landscapes that city leaders understandably condemned.

But he also knew his place and why he had chosen it, the daily activities that kept him sane. He had even stopped wondering how long his chosen path, his deliberate suspension in limbo, would last.

One day at a time, he whispered, a trite and overused adage that nonetheless was a perfect description of his existence.

He reached into his tent and pulled out his backpack. His toolkit, he called it. Large and aluminum-framed, it was the same one he had humped along alpine trails during his recent years of wandering. Like a symbol in a photographic essay, it had been propped against boulders in the Rocky Mountains, sandstone formations in Utah, logs along rivers in the Appalachians, and countless benches in bus and train stations.

He rummaged through it, feeling the small leather pouch that held the alms from St. Francis, and then the series of large metal thermoses. They were top-of-the-line Stanley brand, able to keep the coffee from St. Francis piping hot overnight. Tucked neatly beside them were stacks of paper cups. The accessories for his rounds.

He patted the scratched cell phone in his front pocket, then shook himself again. The morning's first stop would be a woman who had arrived yesterday evening dressed in a T-shirt and board shorts. She was tall, thin, probably in her late 30s. She looked a bit cleaner than others in the encampment, except for her unkempt auburn hair that fell in tangles around her shoulders. With her back turned to him, he had seen a gash on one of her pale, white legs— uncared for, at risk of infection.

He remembered how he had approached her cautiously in the twilight, using the non-threatening body language mastered from years on the street. She had turned quickly to see a tall, lean white man with sinewy muscles, his dark hair disheveled, dressed in threadbare clothes and scuffed shoes. His face, ruggedly handsome, was creased by sun and wind, his stubble of a beard tinged with gray. There were scars visible on his forearms.

He recalled her intense hazel eyes boring into him with a blend of emotions that even he, a man who had specialized in words, could barely describe. They seemed to hold a mixture of fear, defiance, and curiosity all at once.

"What do you want?" she had snapped.

"I don't want anything. I'm offering something."

Her face had contorted with a wry smile.

"Heard that line before."

He had returned her smile gently. "I'm sure you have. It's just that I noticed that gash on the back of your leg. I have a good first aid kit here."

He had lifted it like someone proving his lack of a weapon to the police. She seemed to focus on him, *really* focus. Those inexplicable eyes were also beautiful, and they flickered with a note of resignation.

"I was squeezing through a fence," she had said, "trying to get away from someone's dog. It hurts like hell."

In the end, she had let him clean the wound, slather it with medicated cream, then wrap it in gauze and adhesive tape. She had flinched at his first touch, then relaxed.

Now, following her first night in Freedom Camp, he could see her faded green tent rustling with signs that she was awake. He poured a cup of coffee from one of the thermoses into a paper cup and stood near the flap.

"Hello," he called in a voice loud enough for her to hear but not disturb others. "I've got a cup of coffee here if you want it."

"Who are you?" came the muffled response.

"It's Henry. The one who helped you last night with your leg. How is it feeling?"

There were some seconds of silence.

"Better," she said, then thrust her hand through the flap to receive the steaming brew. As she did, an odor of stale alcohol seeped into the air from a man sleeping a few yards away, and Henry flashed back…

2018, Las Vegas, Nevada.

"Dad...look at that," a girl's voice, always her voice, disembodied, penetrating his blackout. "Disgusting!"

Then the crushing desert heat of Las Vegas, a wall in front of him, the sound of his urine trickling down bricks into the grimy alleyway. And the stench, not only of nearby trash bins, but his own breath, laden with undigested vodka.

His first thought when he turned and saw the family was, "How unlikely." Four of them—a man, a woman, two children—strolling through the streets of downtown. In prior years, that area of Sin City had been so seedy that foot traffic by tourists was rare, but efforts to clean it up and provide attractions like the Fremont Street Experience had sparked a renaissance.

The little girl pointed at him again, despite her dad tugging at her arm.

"Leave the man alone," he said.

Then the girl's gaze locked on him in a different way, as if she was trying to solve a riddle. She had the eyes of an old soul, searching him, probing him, and the expression on her face turned from disgust to something other worldly.

"Are you still standing there?" The woman's voice from inside the tent snapped him back to the present. "Don't start creepin' on me just because I let you help me."

"Wouldn't think of it," he said with a smile. "Take care of yourself."

She grunted in response.

He turned and looked further into the shade of the overpass. Roger, one of the camp's longest residents, was at his usual post, perched in a niche halfway up the concrete embankment, sporting his kente-cloth headband, surveying the camp like a Bedouin shepherd, his skin bronzed in North America via Africa. He was bopping his head to tunes delivered through earbuds. His eclectic library of jazz and gangster rap was saved on a scraped and faded iPod, a possession so prized that he stuffed it down his underwear at night for protection. Like Henry and others fortunate enough to have the luxury of electronic devices, he kept it charged by plugging into public places that didn't ban the homeless from their property.

Henry crawled up and sat next to him as Roger took off his earbuds.

"Mornin'," said Henry. "What's the soundtrack today?"

"Monk. That recording of the Palo Alto Concert in 1968. It still trips me out that Thelonius agreed to play at the request of a 16-year-old high school student. And the janitor was the one who recorded the session! Far out, as we used to say."

Henry nodded, familiar with the famous performance.

"Did I ever tell you," Roger continued, "that I saw him at the Minor Key in Detroit in 1960?"

Henry smiled to himself. Only a dozen times.

"It was epic. I remember Monk getting up during one of Charlie Rouse's sax solos and dancing around the stage. That man was improvisational down to the secret vaults of his soul."

Roger caught Henry's bemused expression and

laughed.

"I know, I know. Told you that a few times. But the best ones are worth repeating."

"True that," said Henry.

"I know you're not a big jazz fan, but that spacy stuff you listen to—Eno, O'Hearn, Wollo, Hammock—I don't get it. It puts me in a trance on the edge of sleep."

"Maybe that's what attracts me to it. I get to self-medicate without going down the road to perdition. It soothes the gorilla before he busts open his cage. Besides, you know I have other genres in my library."

"I know. And I have to admit that your favorite, Harold Budd, plays some nice piano. A little too impressionistic for me, but I see the attraction."

"Eno said he was like an abstract painter trapped in a musician's body."

"That's spot on," said Roger, nodding his head, then looking reflectively into the distance. "One of the things I miss about the old days living in a house is my vinyl collection. You feel me?"

"I do. For me, it would be my books."

Henry envisioned the oak bookcase in the home he had shared with Marsha, its shelves lined with his precious collection. He saw the afternoon light of the Nevada desert refracting through the leaded-glass windows of his study. Marsha found it intriguing that he had read every one of those volumes, absorbing the material for his career as a professor.

"Anyway," said Roger, "let's get this party started."

He pulled an old bronze bell from his rucksack, as if

he'd snatched it from the neck of a Swiss dairy cow. Then he held it above his head and clanged it a few times, the sound echoing along the underpass.

"Hot coffee! Hot coffee!" he yelled, like a hawker at a county fair.

Immediately there was widespread stirring in the camp, people emerging from their tents to come and get their share. They lined up down the sidewalk, single file in what Henry called the "no judgment zone." He reached into his backpack, removing the thermoses and a stack of paper cups, hoping there would be enough.

One by one, the people received their morning caffeine. Henry held the cups and Roger poured. As he handed the offering to each person, Henry made eye contact if they would receive it, trying to show the compassion that was his lodestar, the emotion that gave him his daily reprieve. He was so accustomed to the stench of their unwashed bodies, mingled with his own, that it barely registered. Many of them he'd never seen before; the population of the camp was in constant flux. But others brought back instant memories.

John, the man Henry had taken to the Social Security office to apply for a new card.

Adela, who allowed Henry to talk her down from a fit of rage. She had been throwing her belongings at anyone near her, screaming, "That's for the first time, you motherfucker! That's for the second time! The third, the fourth, the infinity!" Henry was able to calm her, get her some water, and settle her into her tent. That was weeks ago, and today she looked almost peaceful.

Victor, who once sat alongside Henry during a meal at St. Francis recalling how he lost his job at a shuttered factory then drifted through the US, never able to find a sense of belonging. He ended up sitting in a Texas cotton field at dusk, lifting a gun to his head, ready to fire, then falling back and convulsing with sobs. Not glibly, but with his ever present point of reference, Henry told him, "I hear you, man. I've been there."

Towards the end of the line, Henry noticed a tall sunburned white man. There was something about his face that triggered a memory…

2022, the basement of St. Francis Mission.

"My name is Arlen," the man said, "and I'm an alcoholic."

The group members murmured their welcome. Most were old-timers at the noon meeting. They practiced AA tolerance with each other but would privately admit that they had long ago tired of hearing each other's stories. A newcomer perked up their ears. Even Henry leaned forward with anticipation as the man continued to speak.

"I hit bottom, literally, in a gully along Highway 287, about 10 miles northwest of Midlothian, Texas. Came out of a blackout as my truck went off the road and flipped. I can still see it in slow motion, the fifth of vodka from between my legs flying back over my head as I crashed through a fence, hitting an oak tree, settling back. I guess I blacked out again until I heard the Jaws of Life cutting through the cab. Then there was the ambulance ride and the time in the hospital. I think I was there for a week."

The man rocked his head slowly, as if still dispelling a nightmare. "By all rights, I should be dead. Or far worse, I could have killed someone else. No one can tell me it wasn't my Higher Power watching over me, helping me get out of that hospital and into rehab, helping me get accepted to a trade school and landing a decent job. I even have a girlfriend today.

"Five years sober now." He paused and ran his hand through his hair slowly. "I guess the simplest thing I can say is that I am here. I AM HERE. I'm comfortable in my own skin. And I'm so damn grateful."

The man broke down and started crying softly. Henry felt warm tears on his own cheeks. If it had been an evangelical prayer circle, he thought, they might have gathered around Arlen for a laying on of hands. Instead, the woman next to him lightly touched his knee.

Roger tapped Henry's shoulder, bringing him back. "There you go again, brother. Lost in the ozone. Do I need to worry about you?"

Henry shook his head and refocused. "Nah, it's just my overactive brain. It's a gift and a curse."

Roger chuckled and turned back to the receiving line. The thermoses were nearly empty, but they had reached the final resident. It was the woman whose cut he had tended, reaching for her second cup of the morning. She looked at him with curiosity, sizing him up more closely.

"You again," she said with a slight smile.

"Yeah," he replied, meeting her gaze and struck again by the latent beauty of her eyes, accentuated by a wildness in their depths. "What you see is what you get."

She laughed softly, scrutinized him for a few more seconds, then finally walked away with her steaming cup.

"What was that about?" asked Roger.

Henry shrugged. "Who knows? I helped her bandage a cut last night. Anyway, mission accomplished."

They fist-bumped.

"Allah will provide," Roger said with a grin, then grew more serious. "The numbers keep growing. Are you sure you can get enough thermoses in that old backpack? Are you sure your guys at St. Francis will keep working with us?"

"I'm positive. They see it as part of their mission. They're on board with both the coffee and the alms."

The money was a recent addition. Henry carried a personal debit card linked to the remaining funds in an account from his past, but St. Francis had offered petty cash to run errands for those in need. He gratefully accepted the gesture. The medical supplies to doctor the woman's leg had come from that reserve. He kept a small notepad in his backpack where he listed the expenses, and he faithfully turned in the receipts.

As he was restacking the thermoses carefully in his backpack, the shriek of a baby echoed beneath the overpass. It was more than a hunger or dirty diaper cry; it had the stinging ring of pain.

2

"What was that?" Henry exclaimed.

"Not sure," said Roger, "but a new woman and her baby arrived last night. See the blue tent by that column, next to the rusted barrel? That's where she set up."

Henry zipped up his backpack and nestled it next to Roger. "Watch my stuff. I'm going to check it out."

"You got it, brother."

He slid down the embankment and hurried towards the tent. The baby had lapsed into a low set of sobs that seemed unnatural. When he got near, the flap was open, revealing a young woman clutching a little girl to her chest, rocking back and forth. She looked up at Henry with a blend of wariness and desperation.

"Don't be afraid of me," he said, "I'm here to help if I can. What's your name?"

Her eyes met his and she seemed to acquiesce. "Aisha."

"What happened?"

"I'm not sure. Last night after we got here, Tanika's breathing got a little hoarse. I thought it was just the humidity. But now look at her."

The woman held the girl away from her chest. Henry looked down and tried not to let shock register on his face. The child was taking short gasps for air and her lips had a bluish cast. He had seen this once before with a toddler, signs of acute COVID-19 infection.

"We need to get her to the hospital immediately," he said.

Aisha nodded as he pulled out his cellphone and dialed 911. To the city's credit, even a location in Freedom Camp got a quick response, especially since they were near a downtown fire station. The EMTs arrived in five minutes, lights flashing along the underside of the bridge. Two of them brought a stretcher and, after a quick assessment, placed an oxygen mask over Tanika's face.

"You're the mother?" said one of the EMTs to Aisha.

"Yes."

"Come with us in the ambulance."

"Can he come also?" she asked, tilting her head towards Henry.

"Is he the father?"

"No, just a friend."

The EMT looked Henry up and down in a clinical way, his eyes lingering on Henry's scarred forearms.

"No, ma'am, only you're allowed."

"It's all right, Aisha. I'll see you at the hospital," said Henry.

He followed the procession out of the concrete gully

until they reached the ambulance. They loaded Tanika into the back, wrapped in a clean blanket, then Aisha scrambled up behind them. As they pulled away, she leaned towards the back window to wave tentatively at Henry, triggering a painful remembrance…

2018, Las Vegas Nevada.

Marsha's last ambulance ride occurred on a cold Nevada night at 2:00 a.m. Hospice care had allowed Henry to keep her at home during her final days of metastatic breast cancer, but when she began moaning loudly from her pain, he called 911.

He rode with her, holding her hand, heavy with a premonition of the end. In the Hospice Unit of the Valley Hospital Medical Center, the doctor shared some final words.

"It's just a matter of hours," she said with an Indian accent. "Feel free to stay as long as you wish, but don't expect any responses. That said, just remember that hearing is the last sense to go. Whatever you say may indeed get through at some level."

Marsha was heavily sedated with morphine, and her breathing had taken on the death rattle common in a human being's final transition. Early during her illness, Henry had wrangled with the questions of why a woman so intelligent and beautiful, one who had touched the lives of so many in her career as a nurse administrator, could be reduced to skin and bones. No more futile musings. He simply held her hand and wiped her brow with a cold rag, so present in the moment that it seemed razor-edged.

Unlike other men he knew, he had never spared his words or feelings. He regularly told his wife how much he loved her, how much she meant to him on so many levels. He didn't want to leave things unspoken until it was too late. Nonetheless, sitting there alone with her, he poured out his heart once again.

"I know I've said this before, my love, but please—if you can—hear me one last time. Your grace in my life has been a constant warmth and encouragement. Your love has been a brightness I never expected, and perhaps felt I never deserved. Please, please know that I will truly never forget you and all the joy you brought into this world. Into my world."

In the silence that followed, punctuated only by her ragged breathing, had it been real or his imagination? She seemed to softly squeeze his hand.

As he walked along the alley towards the back door of St. Francis, Henry replayed the events of the afternoon.

He had used some alms to take a bus to the hospital, sitting with Aisha as medical personnel worked on Tanika. The diagnosis was indeed COVID-19, but they were able to stabilize the child and bring her blood oxygen level back to normal. The doctors were optimistic.

While Tanika slept in the pediatric ICU, Henry took Aisha to the basement cafeteria and bought her some food. Despite her anxiety, she ate like it was her last meal. Afterwards, in the waiting room, he heard her story, one that was sadly familiar. Living as a single woman in the city, involvement with a young man who promised his loyalty but disappeared before Tanika's birth, the decision not to abort, then postpartum depression, the loss of her minimum wage job, a gradual descent to the street. He had listened without interrupting, then assured her he would check in on her and Tanika regularly.

He reached the back door of St. Francis and used their password knock—three, two, one. It took a moment before Arturo opened the door. He was a St. Francis success story, an unemployed chef who had fallen to the street because of drug use, then found his way to one of the cots at the shelter. He had gotten clean and stayed on as a volunteer, gradually working his way to a paid position as manager of the center's food services.

He reached out his hand to shake Henry's, his arm sleeved with tattoos. Steam from the kitchen's dishwasher billowed around his head.

"Hey, Henry. What's your day been like?

"Eventful. An infant in the camp needed emergency care. Fortunately, it looks like she'll be OK."

Arturo held Henry's eyes for a second, a smile lighting up his face.

"What's fortunate is that they had you nearby."

Henry shrugged and returned the smile, briefly letting a sense of satisfaction fill his empty interior.

"Anyway," said Arturo, "let's get you hooked up."

Henry slipped off his backpack with the empty thermoses, then handed it to Arturo along with the alms pouch and receipts. It only took a few moments before Arturo returned with new provisions.

"Namaste, God bless you, as-salamu alaykum," said

27

Arturo with a chuckle, using the blend of salutations that was their daily ritual.

"Mitakuye oyasin, may the Force be with you, keep on truckin'!" said Henry.

They both laughed, bumped fists, then Henry turned and departed. As Arturo watched him recede down the alley, a volunteer in the kitchen came up alongside him, a young man named Brad. Sirens bayed in the distance.

"What do you really know about that guy?"

"Not a lot," said Arturo. "For quite a while, every time I asked him where he came from, he just said, 'I'm making the rounds.' Then he opened up a bit more and shared that he had been drifting around the country. He stayed in campgrounds, cheap hotels, and homeless encampments. I didn't find out his last name, Thornwood, until one of the nuns told me. She had spoken to him when he stayed here a few days."

"Henry Thornwood," said Brad, as if speaking the words put flesh on the man.

"Yep. I Googled his name and the only thing I found was an old LinkedIn listing for a professor at the University of Nevada, Las Vegas. He taught American and English literature. The photo was taken about 5 years ago, so now he's probably in his early 40s. He looked a lot different, cleaned up and all, but it was definitely him. Then he seemed to drop off the face of the earth."

"That man has some mileage on him."

Arturo sighed. "Don't we all."

"I get this powerful vibe when I look at him," said Brad.

"A vibe?"

"Yeah. I don't quite know how to describe it. Sort of fierce, like there's something beneath the surface that's unpredictable. Know what I mean?"

"I do. That's perfect. And it fits with what I've heard from others who have stayed here at St. Francis. I guess shortly after his arrival in the city, he found a young punk trying to rob a woman's tent while she was still in it. He laid the guy flat and some others had to hold him back or it might have been worse. No one fucks with him, which is perfect for the kind of service he does on a daily basis."

"Badass," said Brad.

Arturo chuckled. "Yep. A badass dude in a badass world."

Henry sat perched on the edge of the overpass above Freedom Camp. It was near midnight, but many of the camp's denizens were still active, chattering with each other or with the voices in their heads. Two small fires poured acrid smoke into the night.

He had his earbuds on, listening to *How Close Your Soul* by Robin Guthrie and Harold Budd. The day's clouds had cleared, and as he gazed up at the night sky, his feet dangling over the edge, he drifted back to another night, another place…

2018, Spring Mountains, Nevada.
The Milky Way was stunning in the desert sky, lights that had streamed their radiance for up to billions of years. He was sitting on a precipice near the summit of

Mt. Charleston. He had spent the day hiking there—past the ancient bristlecone pines that predated Christ; past the wrecked fuselage of a CIA plane that crashed in 1955, killing 14 passengers. He made his camp just a few feet from the edge that dropped off sharply into Carpenter Canyon.

He leaned forward until vertigo swept over him. Then he leaned back until his spine rested on stones still warm from the day's sunlight. Rocking forward and back, forward and back, not yet executing his intent for this hike, but simply pondering a phrase he had read in an interview with Francis Weller: "The work of the mature person is to carry grief in one hand, gratitude in the other, and to be stretched large by them."

He was tired, so tired of the stretching, and it had become increasingly difficult to find gratitude, the grief like a gray fog in which everything seemed to be equidistant and uninspiring.

He leaned forward again over the precipice, the abyss with its promise of ending all the pain. Then, again, back to the solid earth beneath his back.

"Am I just afraid to let go?" he whispered to himself.

A bright shooting star arced over his head towards the horizon.

An ambulance siren snapped him back to the present. Someone down in the camp was yelling, "It's time! Can't you see! It's time!"

He leaned forward until the dizziness surged through his body like a rush of 100 proof whiskey. Then he leaned back and felt the warm sidewalk on his back.

"Don't worry, my love," he whispered. "Tomorrow we will make the rounds for one more day."

3

Henry awoke to someone rustling the flap of his tent, then starting to unzip it. His eyes shot open and he sat upright on his sleeping bag, fists clenched for a fight. He then relaxed as he saw the woman whose cut he had cleaned peering through the opening. She had brushed her hair and cleaned herself up. She looked down at him with a determined expression.

"That's a dangerous thing to do on the street," he said with an edge of anger. "I might have smashed you in the face."

"No," she said, "I don't think so, not after I saw you passing out coffee yesterday. Anyway, get up. I want to help you. I need something to do."

Both startled and a bit amused by the woman's boldness, Henry slipped on his clothes, noticing that she continued to watch him.

"I guess it would be OK for you to help," he said, fumbling self-consciously with his belt. "You're obviously feeling better."

"That's a relative state of mind, but yeah, compared to yesterday, I've come back a bit into the land of the living."

"You know that my name's Henry. What's yours?"

"Cindy. Cindy Rhodes."

"How's your leg?"

"It's improved. It doesn't seem to be infected. And I wanted to ask you about that. Who are you? Some self-appointed guardian angel for the homeless?"

He got up, unzipped the flap more fully, and slid out, careful not to touch her as he stood. At first he avoided her intense gaze, then he looked her squarely in the eyes.

"No angel, that's for sure. But self-appointed? Sort of. I'm assisted by the people at the St. Francis shelter. Call it what you want. It's my way of staying sane and sober until I discover if there's a next chapter in my life."

"If?"

"Yeah, if."

She lifted her eyebrows, not in derision, but as a sign of acceptance. "That's always the question, isn't it? When I wake up at night and replay the events of my life, the words 'what if?' attack me like a swarm of mosquitoes."

He looked away. He had been cornered by too many people on the upswing of their bipolar disorder or riding a speeding meth train, babbling at him until it felt like ants were crawling under his skin. Would this woman, Cindy, be one of them?

His eyes scanned the encampment. New residents had moved in during the night, a few in tents, others with no shelter. One Black man was seated in a lotus position on his sleeping bag, his palms pressed together in what Henry knew was the Hindu gesture of *Anjali mudra*, as if the guy was saying namaste to a new day. Sunlight broke through shifting clouds and the ubiquitous smell of a trashcan fire rode on a soft breeze.

"Yeah," said Henry finally, appreciating that Cindy had waited in silence for his answer. Maybe she was tolerable. "What if? The tenuous thread of my life, one day at a time, leaning between being and not being."

Cindy's eyes narrowed, searching his face again as if for a clue. "That's an odd and refreshing blast of honesty. It's also a bit scary."

Henry shrugged and reached inside the tent, retrieving his backpack with the thermoses and cups, then hoisting it onto his shoulders.

"If you're going to help today, I need to check with Roger. I don't want him to feel replaced. We've been partners for a while."

Cindy nodded. "Works for me."

"Then let's go."

They walked toward the underpass where Roger was already sitting in his niche. As they neared, he pulled out his earbuds and watched them approach.

"What's on the playlist today?" asked Henry

"Felt in the mood for some fusion. *Romantic Warrior* by Chick Corea and Return to Forever."

"I know that piece," said Henry. "Stanley Clarke's bass work is over the top."

"Yeah, so fine. And Al Di Meola is a master on the

frets. Fusion at its best."

Roger turned his gaze to Cindy with a questioning arch of his brows.

"This is Cindy," said Henry. "She got here a couple days ago and would like to assist us."

Roger smiled and nodded.

"Sure. We can always use more help. Where did you drift in from, Cindy?"

"I was in San Francisco for a while until I got tired of the fog. Most recently, I lived in a community along the Columbia River."

Roger nodded. "I hear you about the city by the bay. I stayed there during the summer once and Mark Twain was right when he said, 'the coldest winter I ever spent was a summer in San Francisco.' Don't blame you for hittin' the road. Welcome to our crew."

He shifted his attention to Henry.

"Let's get this gig started."

As usual, Roger's bell summoned the residents of Freedom Camp to rise and start forming a queue.

"Y'all can make two lines today," he said in a loud voice. "We've got some extra help."

Roger poured the cups while Cindy and Henry handed them out, the sounds of traffic, horns, and a distant siren providing an urban soundtrack. Some of the men and women said thanks as they received their cups; others averted their eyes. As usual, the cloying odor of unwashed humanity assaulted Henry's nostrils. Access to fresh water and toilets was one of the greatest deprivations of living on the street. Henry had encountered a couple tent cities where city officials, in partnership with charities, offered porta-potties and hygiene stations for showers. But that was rare. The folks at St. Francis allowed Henry to bathe a couple times a week, and he felt a bit guilty for accessing his privilege.

He watched Cindy out of the corner of his eye as she passed out her allotment. She said "good morning" to each person and, for the first time, Henry saw her fully smile. It transformed her face, giving her a deeper beauty that he instantly appreciated. One older woman who walked with a cane had difficulty grasping the cup in her arthritic palm, so Cindy helped curl her swollen fingers around it until it was secure.

Cindy sensed that he was watching her and she turned to look him in the eyes. She smiled again and Henry felt a stirring inside that had not been there for years.

4

Cindy continued to help for the rest of the week, and she and Henry grew more comfortable with each other. One afternoon, he went to check on Tanika and Aisha, choosing to walk rather than ride the bus. Cindy insisted on joining him for the 10-block trek through downtown. The morning's clouds had dissolved and the humidity was intense. Cindy seemed to be feeling better each day, a spring in her step as she kept stride with him.

"Do you always walk this fast?" she chided.

"I do. You want me to slow down?'

"Not at all. It's nice to find someone with a pace like mine."

They came to an intersection with a red light, and as they waited for it to flash green, Henry read the message on the digital billboard of a bank across the street. *Time is not money. Don't squander it.*

Cindy laughed. "I love it. Daily inspiration from an institution that only wants your cash."

The walk sign flashed, and when they got to the other side, they fell again into a quick rhythm, the hospital looming on the block ahead. They made their way through the entrance and took the elevator to the pediatric wing. As Henry had expected, they found Aisha in the lounge area. She turned her head towards them and immediately broke into a smile.

"Hey Henry, Tanika is much better today. They'll probably discharge her tomorrow."

Aisha shifted her gaze to Cindy.

"This is Cindy," said Henry. "She's been helping me with errands today."

"Hello," said Cindy as Aisha nodded.

"So what are you two? Social workers in disguise? Do you come from some agency or church? I hope you're not going to start handing me religious pamphlets."

Henry chuckled. "No, we're just people who know what it feels like to live on the street."

"Well," said Aisha, "if you believe in God, and I do even after everything that's happened to me, you were sent by the Almighty at just the right time. I don't know what I would've done. I was panicking."

She unexpectedly stood and gave Henry a hug, which he stiffly returned. Then Aisha turned to Cindy.

"I don't even know you, girl, but bless you also for being someone who cares."

Both Henry and Aisha saw the tears that immediately began to stream down Cindy's cheeks.

Over the next couple of days, in addition to serving

coffee, Henry and Cindy secured insulin for a man in the encampment and fixed the tears in a couple tents with duct tape that Henry kept in his backpack. After being essentially alone for so many years, he was surprised by how much he enjoyed Cindy's company. Their conversation was casual, nothing too deep yet, but he found it pleasant. That in itself was a surprise, since he normally avoided small talk. He had even introduced Cindy to Arturo, securing a shower for her at St. Francis.

Around dusk one evening, they splurged on a couple sandwiches using Henry's debit card, then sat together on top of the overpass at his usual perch. Rush hour traffic had waned, but the white noise of the city still surrounded them.

Henry swallowed a mouthful. "I'm impressed by how you work with the people, like that woman with the arthritic hands you helped on the first day."

Cindy didn't look at him, just chewed her food and surveyed the encampment below. "How come you have a debit card? Most people on the street have to panhandle to get some spending money."

"It's a long story. I don't burden people with my sad history."

"I can walk away if I want. Try me."

He was silent for a moment and Cindy had the courtesy not to prompt him any further.

"Here's the synopsis. I was an associate professor at the University of Nevada, Las Vegas, part of the graduate school of humanities. I was married to a woman named Marsha who had a successful career as a nurse administrator. We had our differences like any couple, but mostly we were deeply in love."

He stopped, took a bite of his sandwich, fighting the impulse to get up and walk away. *What am I doing?* Instead, when he noticed the intensity with which Cindy was listening, he continued.

"She died of metastatic breast cancer. I always had some trouble with drinking, slipping in and out of AA, smart enough to know when I needed a booster shot of help, but dumb enough to keep dabbling in denial. After she was gone, I didn't give a damn anymore. Everything, especially my state of mind, was shrouded in darkness. I was like Nicholas Cage in *Leaving Las Vegas*, except my suicide by alcohol was less intentional. I left my job after numerous students reported seeing me tipsy or hungover in class, and then I ended up being arrested for drunk and disorderly behavior in downtown Vegas."

The incident with the girl in the Vegas alleyway flashed again through his mind.

"The court mandated a treatment center, and while I was in there I had a real estate agent sell our house. The debit card is linked to what's left of the money Marsha and I saved during our marriage. I might have another year to go if I'm careful, but after that, who knows."

"How long ago did Marsha die?"

"A little over five years."

Cindy chewed her food thoughtfully. "Did you get sober?"

"I did, and it was strange and unexpected. The other guys I went through treatment with were mostly sentenced from prison or picked up off the street like me. Vagrants and cons were my support group and I grew to love them. They became my band of brothers. It's like they say. Addiction is the great equalizer. It has no respect for age, race, class, or education. It's a lesson I carry with me at all times."

Cindy nodded. "That's a rough road, but I still don't understand. You had money. Why did you end up on the street after getting out of rehab?"

"I was supposedly on sabbatical, but I knew I'd never go back. I decided to take an extended backpacking trip to see the US. I rode trains and buses. I walked and I hitchhiked. I went to national parks and state parks, but when my travels took me through cities, I couldn't help but notice the homeless encampments. There's an old cliché that they drill into you during recovery. 'There but for the grace of God go I.' It opened my eyes more widely every day to people on the streets."

He took a deep breath, still wondering why he was spilling his guts, but feeling some relief in doing so.

"One day, I was in Washington Square Park in New Orleans, looking at the faces on its AIDS memorial. It's a dramatic sculpture, showing the faces of people who died from that plague. Nearby, there was this drunk guy passed out on the sidewalk, so I went over and shook him to see if he was OK. He looked up at me and it's hard to describe what I felt. I was looking at myself. At the bottom I had hit it my own life. But it was more than that. The humanity of that guy's eyes, even in his filthy state, was an epiphany. I could see his condition was serious. He was having trouble breathing and all he could whisper was 'help me.'"

"What did you do?"

"I used my cell phone to call an ambulance, and it's lucky I did. He had acute alcohol poisoning and probably would have died. I followed up with him until they placed him in a New Orleans' rehab center, but who knows where he is today."

Henry sighed. "His name was Alex. You probably think this is weird, but I need to say his name out loud every once in a while. Alex."

He rubbed his hand over his face. Someone was singing from the encampment below, a tune that Henry recognized as *Set Fire to the Rain* by Adele. Like so many surreal moments on the street, it made him smile.

"The strangest thing happened as I helped Alex. The darkness I could never shake following Marsha's death was pushed back a bit. Not gone, but more tolerable. I started intentionally looking for people I could help on my travels and I've been doing that ever since. Like I said, the money in my account is pretty low now, but I'm going to play this out to whatever ending is in store."

"That's a lot," said Cindy.

She was silent for a moment, digesting what he'd said. "I'm curious. Most recovery programs are spiritual. They talk about a higher power, and you said, 'there but for the grace of God go I.' Do you believe in a god?"

"No, I don't. And I honestly say that with some sadness. I've listened to countless people talk about how their higher powers helped them with one problem after another. I can't get there. It seems like wishful thinking at best, delusion at worst. But I can say this. My higher power is finding a way to be useful and serve the common good. I guess I've always agreed with Sartre. In the face of life's absurdity and the crushing certainty of death, we can either kill ourselves and end the pain, or find some way to bring meaning to our lives. Even if, as Camus said, it's like Sisyphus pushing his stone up a hill day after day after day."

Cindy chuckled. "You have a way with words, professor. I bet you were a great teacher. You have a depth that's not just bookish but based in real life. I always looked for that with my college instructors, but it was rare."

He shrugged. "I wasn't that seasoned during my tenure. But I am grateful for what I'm continuing to learn. Thanks for helping me see that."

"You mentioned suicide in the thoughts of that philosopher. Have you ever thought about killing yourself?"

Henry was struck by her bluntness. "More times than you can imagine. It's part of the reason I sit here every night."

Her eyebrows arched quizzically. "What do you mean?"

He told her about his trip to Mt. Charleston, his perch above the canyon, his reluctance to follow through with his original plan, snared in that limbo that he never seemed able to escape.

"I remember that moment each night as I rock back and forth over this ledge. It reminds me of my daily choice."

"Jesus," she said. "Don't be offended, but that seems masochistic. You remind yourself *every day* about hanging between life and death?"

He shrugged, feeling a bit defensive. "I am what I am. But enough about me. It's only fair that I get to hear your story as well. How did you end up on this overpass with a guy you just met, listening to his existential sob story?"

She didn't hesitate. "The simple answer is depression. I don't mean just a few passing weeks of sadness. It's been longer, almost crushing me at times."

"That's hard to imagine given the vitality I've seen in you this week."

"What you see is someone clawing her way back."

"Are you willing to share it?"

"I guess so," she said, taking a last bite of her sandwich, then chewing thoughtfully before proceeding.

"I was living in Huntington Beach, California. I had gotten an MBA degree with dreams of starting my own business, but I fell into selling real estate, specializing in high-end homes. It was good money, so I stayed with it. My husband Kevin and I had known each other since high school and there was this expectation from both sides of our families was that we would get married and have children."

She paused and took a breath. "Those are the thoughts that haunt me. The choices we make. The choices *I* made, setting events into motion that I never anticipated."

"What kind of work did Kevin do?"

"He built a successful HVAC company. We would probably still be together, but he had a serious gambling addiction behind the scenes. I guess I didn't want to see how bad it was getting. Both partners can be in denial. Plus, I had gotten pregnant for the first time. I had my hands full with morning sickness and managing a few property appointments."

She shook her head. "Like an idiot, I never separated our business accounts. In just two days while I was at a conference, Kevin went on a binge and drained almost everything we had. As usual, he was super apologetic. He kept promising he would make things right, but I was feeling more and more depressed. I couldn't bring in as much money, and the bank ended up foreclosing on our mortgage."

Henry noticed her breathing was getting shallower, and she began to clench and unclench her fists. A man was shuffling slowly on the sidewalk below, pausing every few feet to point into the air and shout, "Buzzards!"

"You don't have to tell me the rest."

"No," she said. "You shared your story with me. It's only fair."

She took a deep breath, calming herself. "Like I said, we were pretty much broke. I was six months pregnant, and Kevin began to be verbally abusive, flying off the handle for the slightest reason. I usually went into my bedroom and ignored him, which angered him even more. He would follow me and bang on my door, or open it and stand there shouting at me."

Her voice grew hoarse with emotion. "One evening he didn't return from work until very late. I imagined him borrowing money to gamble some more, maybe even from illegal sources, and my rage took over. When he finally came in around midnight, I was pissed. I started screaming and yelling and throwing books at him. Then he suddenly attacked me, hitting me over and over again until I blacked out."

Henry felt his own fists clenching, his mind racing through numerous memories when he had defended both women and men on the streets, never backing down, a fierceness in his eyes that made others finally look away.

"Motherfucker," he muttered. "Damn him."

Cindy's teeth were clenched. "Damnation's too lenient for Kevin. I woke up on the floor, then crawled to my phone and called 911. I ended up at the hospital and I lost our baby. I watched as they delivered her almost fully-formed from my womb but limp and lifeless. We were going to name her Sarah."

Her jaw unclenched and she started to cry, softly but steadily. Henry instinctively put his hand on her shoulder. She flinched, then allowed him to rest it there. He didn't prod her to continue, just let her cry, her head hung to her chest. Someone's car alarm went off in the distance, beeping persistently.

Finally, she wiped her eyes and took a breath. "The police got him for assault and resisting arrest. While he was in jail, a public defender asked me if I wanted to press charges. I knew I would have to testify and relive all that trauma, so I told him I wanted to wait and think about it. He warned me that Kevin could be set free without those charges, especially since he claimed I attacked him first. I didn't care. I was sick of our whole mess. I just wanted to cut and run, to get as far away from him and my former life as possible. A social worker helped me transfer to a battered woman's organization that ran a string of secret safe houses, and they placed me in a home a couple cities over from where I lived."

"How long were you there?"

"About three months. They were so kind to me. Like angels. I attended their daily support groups and tried to put on a good face. But a number of the women had children with them, and it kept bringing back the pain of losing Sarah. More and more, I felt that burning desire to run. That's when I met a volunteer counselor who talked about a commune in the forest near the Columbia River Gorge. She had gone there during the toughest time of her life and it had given her some healing."

"You went there?"

"I did. I left my car in the garage of a friend named Vanessa who swore she wouldn't tell anyone. I took my only remaining cash from a small personal savings account and worked my way up the coast on bus rides. I stopped for a while in San Francisco, then made it to the commune. But I was always looking over my shoulder. I was always afraid that Kevin would somehow track me down."

"He would do that?"

"Definitely. You should have seen his eyes when he attacked me. He's possessed by something that needs to be vented on others. He's changed so much from the man I first knew. Plus, he owns a couple handguns. 'Just for target practice,' he always says, but he has the permits and he's trained in how to use them."

She scanned the encampment below. "The commune I went to is called Tamanass. It's owned and run by a woman named Jean who sold a string of successful businesses and bought some land in the woods. She rents trailers and tiny homes on the property. The community supports itself in a bunch of ways. They sell vegetables and flowers from their large garden. Others collect mushrooms from the forest and deliver them to restaurants in the city."

"You told Roger that's where you were most recently."

She nodded.

"Why did you leave?"

She hesitated. "I don't know if I should get into that since you're an alcoholic."

"What do you mean?"

"Don't they tell you to stay away from any kind of mind-altering substance?"

He chuckled. "Why? Are you going to offer me some crank or pull out a flask of whiskey?"

She smiled. "Fair enough. Tamanass has a ceremony once a month using ayahuasca the way Native Americans use peyote. They never pressured me to be part of it, but my curiosity overcame me, especially when I heard others say it had helped them with trauma and depression. Do you know anything about ayahuasca?"

"Oddly, I do. I had a student who wrote a paper about her experiences with it in Peru. Sort of an unusual approach for an assignment on Joseph Conrad, but hey, I always encouraged freedom of expression. I know that the brew they use in ceremonies is made from two plants, one of them containing the DMT that leads to hallucinations. My student cited a book called *Cosmic Serpent* by a man who drew parallels between the cellular structure of the ayahuasca vine, the helix of human DNA, and the serpent image found in mythical stories of the Andes. I even learned a new word. Entheogen. Substances that scientists can't really dissect completely but are known to cause mystical states of awareness. My first impulse was to dismiss it all as rubbish, but I definitely found it intriguing. Her paper was excellent. She made an analogy between Kurtz exploring his heart of darkness and her own willingness to go deeper into her own psyche."

Cindy wiped the tears from her cheek and smiled a bit brighter. "Whoa, professor, that brain of yours is crammed with facts."

Someone in the encampment had lit a trashcan fire that was larger than usual. Black smoked billowed up past the height of the overpass to their left. *Fool*, thought Henry, *why not just send smoke signals to the authorities?*

"I went to the ceremony for a few months," Cindy continued.

"And?"

"I felt like I was close to a breakthrough about my miscarriage. Jean encouraged me to stay the course, but it was too painful and I did my usual thing. I ran away. When I got here, I pitched my tent in another encampment before coming to this one. I don't have enough funds to rent a room for any length of time. The truth is, I didn't know what to do. I don't know where I'm going or what's going to happen with my life."

She laid on her back, seemingly done with her story. Henry leaned back also. Then, through force of habit, he raised himself back up and leaned vertiginously over the edge, looking down at Freedom Camp. Suddenly, he felt Cindy's hand threading its way into his. The touch felt both alien and welcome, opening vaults of repressed memories.

"Look at us," Cindy said, "teetering between the past and the future, between life and death."

She suddenly laughed and pulled him back to the pavement. Then they rocked back and forth, back and forth, as sirens called from the depths of the city.

5

Henry said goodnight to Cindy at the flap of her tent, crawled into his own, then eased back on his sleeping pad. He heard her rustling in her tent.

He couldn't sleep. The events of the day and their conversation had his mind racing. As he thought of Aisha's relief over Tanika's recovery and Cindy's tears as she recounted her miscarriage, a memory returned...

2017, Las Vegas, Nevada.

"The results came back negative," Marsha said. "I'm not sure we can afford to go any further, either financially or emotionally."

For two years, after failing to get pregnant naturally, they had been trying in vitro ferritization, sharing a desire to raise at least one child together.

"Are you giving up the idea of parenthood completely?" he asked.

"Not necessarily. We could always adopt."

Henry looked at her with surprise. Marsha was an adoptee, and the process of researching her birth parents and connecting with them had been emotionally draining.

"Are you sure about that with everything you've gone through?

"Only if you're open to it."

"I am," he said. "I think it could be wonderful."

He reached over to take her hand, and the memory of her hand reminded him of Cindy's warm fingers in his own just a short time earlier.

In her own tent, Cindy was fitful. Throughout her life, when she had divulged intimate details with others, the effect had been cathartic, lifting a load from her mind. Sharing with Henry had the opposite effect. Reliving Kevin's attack had riled her so much that her skin crawled. It was a new experience to feel such a deep and dark anger. She had always repressed that emotion, wearing a mask fit for the public. But now she was imagining, even relishing, scenarios of revenge. She saw herself inflicting violence on Kevin by smashing his face until it was bloody. She imagined him in prison being sexually and physically abused by other inmates.

What's become of me? she wondered.

She turned her thoughts to Henry. She hadn't told him the most painful part of her time at Tamanass. Her final experiment with ayahuasca had shaken her to her core, especially one image that haunted her daily. It was the reason she had fled, a pain so acute that she could only skirt around it. If this was PTSD, it opened up a new level of empathy for everyone who suffered from it.

She heard rustling noises from Henry's tent. He was highly intelligent, and she had enjoyed their conversation. She even liked how he lapsed in to mini-lectures, as if he was addressing a class full of students. It didn't seem self-absorbed, just his natural way of expressing himself. And it allowed her to use a fuller range of her own vocabulary, something that had atrophied during her years with Kevin.

But Henry's decision to continue living on the streets confounded her. She certainly understood how grief could drive you to despair. She also knew that the damaging effects of alcoholism lingered inside a person even in sobriety. She had heard someone describe it as putting a plant in a dark cupboard and trying to forget about it, only to discover later that it was growing all the time, ready to attack like the shrubs in *Little Shop of Horrors*. Another person told her that though the disease may seem out of sight, out of mind, it's doing pushups in the dark, staying strong, waiting for a chance to pounce.

Was Henry's unresolved grief and his background of addiction like a time bomb waiting to explode?

The last thing I need is another addict in my life, she thought. *The last thing I need is to bear the brunt of someone's anger.*

Still, she kept thinking of him. Despite the trauma he had shared, he radiated a strength that attracted her, even with his disheveled appearance. There had a been a couple men at Tamanass who made overtures to her, but she felt walled away and remote. The experience with Kevin was too recent, too vivid. Like many of the women she had met in the safe house, she wondered if she would ever trust a man again. More pointedly, would she ever *want* to?

Being around Henry felt different. At least so far, there was no energy coming from him that expected something from her. Nothing predatory. Even though their past experiences were vastly different, they had exchanged their stories like equals, one human being to another. She looked forward to seeing him in the morning. She even looked forward to what might develop between them in the days ahead.

Look at me, she thought, a smile spreading over her face. *Fantasizing about a man in a homeless encampment.*

She finally fell asleep, and it wasn't long before the vision replayed itself. Always that face, otherworldly, the eyes staring straight into hers, the lips moving, speaking something she needed to hear, and her refusal to listen. Then the turning, the running away blindly, the searing pain in her mind and heart.

She let out a small yelp and awakened. A light rain was pattering on the tent and she heard horns blaring in the distance, leading her to think of Kevin and where he might be at that moment.

6

Three months earlier

Kevin adjusted the binoculars from his vantage point on a nearby hill, focusing on the backyard of a suburban home in a Southern California beach community. He had parked his car a safe distance away and walked, not wanting to arouse suspicion. This was the third and final location he had scouted over the past months, and though his hopes weren't high, he was determined to execute his plan.

After the furious fight with Cindy, looking at her lying unconscious on the ground, he panicked and fled. His rage, pent-up for years, had exploded like a hair-trigger assault rifle, and he realized he must have partially blacked out, because he barely remembered how many times he had struck her.

But she deserved it, was his cold rationalization, growing icier by the day. *Always playing superior, treating me like I'm handicapped or a nut job she barely tolerates. Withholding affection and acting smug. She's been like that for years!*

Immediately after the attack, he fled their home and hid in a back room of his HVAC company. When the police caught up with him, he was sleeping on a cot. They slammed on the door, announcing they had a warrant, and before he could even shake off his sleep they had broken through the entrance, weapons drawn. That's when he made his second big mistake, resisting arrest by throwing a table lamp and swinging a few punches. They quickly subdued him with a stun gun that felt like a thousand razor blades penetrating his skin.

He knew he was lucky they had only tased him and not used lethal force. After they read him his rights, he discovered that his beating of Cindy had led to the death of their baby. That was the moment he knew how profound his rage had become, because part of him felt some grief, but his overwhelming response was that he was not primarily to blame. *Cindy was! She was the one who had started yelling and throwing things at him!* He could see it clearly in his mind's eyes, her face contorted with anger as well as that pity he had come to loathe.

It was also that moment when he became determined to find her. To force her to understand her role in all of this and take some responsibility. There would be a reckoning with her, one way or another.

He was appointed a public defender, a short guy in a wrinkled suit with disheveled hair and glasses that kept slipping down his nose. Visiting Kevin during his time in jail, he said that since Cindy hadn't pressed charges, they could claim she started the violence and Kevin was simply defending himself. They could also pledge his commitment to treatment for his gambling addiction, which the lawyer felt they should divulge.

During the arraignment, the judge was unmoved, focusing not only the severity of Kevin's assault, but also that he had resisted arrest. Kevin received a sentence of 20 more days in jail, a $10,000 fine, two years of probation, and the order to attend both Gambler's Anonymous and anger management classes. They also slapped a restraining order on him, prohibiting him from coming anywhere near Cindy. He sat impassively, fixing a neutral expression on his face, not wanting to fuel the judge's wrath by any indication of the anger smoldering inside him. Afterwards, Kevin's business partner, Steve, helped secure a bail bond from their operating funds, even though he had become increasingly skeptical of Kevin's erratic behavior.

Kevin returned home to find that Cindy had vanished, taking only one suitcase and a small assortment of clothes. Her Honda was gone, but there was something she didn't know. He had secretly installed LoJack, wondering if she might be cheating on him during her attendance at conferences. The device included an app that let him track her location. He brought it up on his phone, scrolled through her movements, and when he Googled the latest address, it was the administrative offices for Safe Haven, a nonprofit that helped battered women. He knew their staff would be suspicious of any man poking around, no matter how innocent he acted, so he cruised the building in the evening after work, surveying it from different angles. He could see a large parking lot in the rear, hidden by a fence so that only the roofs of a few cars were visible from the street. That barrier continued around the back, concealing the property from a rear alleyway.

He had parked at a distance around dusk and walked down the alley, using a ballcap to shield his face in case there were security cameras. He found a small peephole where one of the knots in the wooden fence had fallen through. Sure enough. Peering into the lot, he was able to see Cindy's late model Honda Civic parked among the other vehicles.

Gotcha, he thought, but then he ran through logistics. He had learned online through a newspaper article that the nonprofit ran a string of safehouses in local communities, their locations zealously guarded.

How would he find those places? If he did, what was he going to do? Break in and demand a meeting with her? That would quickly land him back in jail, this time with slimmer chances for bail.

First things first. After work each day, he positioned himself in different spots around the nonprofit offices, staying a short time each outing, avoiding any pattern that might arouse suspicion. Over the course of a few weeks, he noticed an older model beige Toyota that came and went at various hours after dusk, as if using the cloak of twilight. Through his binoculars, he noticed the same woman driving the car, sometimes alone, at other times with a female passenger.

One evening, he followed the car, making sure to stay back and avoid detection. It was only the woman driver, no passenger, so he wondered if she was simply going home. Instead, the Toyota took three different routes, stopping and pulling into the garages of modest ranch homes in communities miles apart. The car would disappear into the garage, coming out a short time later. She was obviously checking in or running errands. The important point, the victory, was that he now had three places he could surveil.

He wiped his blurry eyes and peered through the binoculars again. Since this was the third home he had staked out, he was beginning to lose hope that he would find her. Maybe she hadn't entered the protection of one of these homes, but had fled to parts unknown, leaving her car behind.

Then suddenly, there she was, walking from the back of the house and sitting down at a wooden picnic table with another woman. They were deeply engrossed in conversation. His binoculars were so powerful that he could see Cindy's lips moving, her hand brushing at her hair.

A smile spread over his face.

7

"The city orders you to vacate this camp! Anyone who loiters is subject to arrest!"

The blaring words, voiced through a bullhorn, rang out in Freedom Camp, awakening Henry at the crack of dawn. He stuck his head outside his tent. To his left, at the furthest edge of the encampment, about a dozen police officers holding nightsticks were picking their way through the maze of tents, sleeping bags, and smoldering trashcans. He heard a man yelling "You heartless motherfuckers!"

Even though he had dreaded this, Henry wasn't surprised. Normally the city posted flyers that warned of impending resettlements. Sometimes they even sent city officials in advance to circulate among residents and suggest alternate places to stay. But times were changing, politicians caving into pressures, and this abrupt raid was symptomatic of the shifting cultural climate, both here and in other cities across the country.

Cindy stuck her head out of her tent. "What's going

on?"

"They're making a sweep. We have to move. Pack up your stuff. Quickly."

Cindy sprang into action as the phalanx of officers got closer. Henry clenched his fists, gritted his teeth, and faced them with a menacing expression. The stance came naturally to him now, almost involuntary.

"Why are you rousting us without any advance notice?" he yelled at the nearest officer. "People need time to find somewhere else to stay!"

To his credit, the officer remained peaceful, leaving his nightstick at his side and looking calmly at Henry. "Don't make us the enemy. This encampment has been reported for fire hazards, drug dealing, even suspected human trafficking. We're just doing our jobs. We don't want anyone to get harmed."

Henry's anger only increased. The lyrics of a Rage Against the Machine song popped into his head. *Now you do what they told ya. Now you do what they told ya.*

"It's not right," he said, spitting out the bitter words as he began to raise one of his fists. "If you had ever been homeless, you might have a shred of…"

He suddenly felt a hand restraining his arm and a soft voice whispering in his ear.

"Don't push it, Henry. Come with me."

It was Cindy, her body pressed firmly into his from behind. He let out his breath like the snort of a horse.

"It's all right, officers," she said in a placating tone. "Give us a few moments and we'll clear out."

"Thank you, ma'am," the officer said, nonplussed by

Henry's reaction, then moving further into the encampment, lifting his bullhorn again.

Henry turned around to confront Cindy. "Clear out? You spend a few days with us and now you're an expert on other places to stay?"

Cindy took one of his hands and held it firmly. "I hear you. But I have an idea. Come with me to Tamanass. I have enough money for two bus tickets. I know that Jean will let us pitch our tents where I stayed in mine. We don't have be there for long, just enough time to get our bearings."

"But I thought you burned your bridges. I thought you put that place in your rearview mirror for good."

"Maybe. I don't know. I don't even know how they'll react if I return. But I was running way out of fear. After our talk last night, I realize I have unfinished business there. Who knows? You might also find some healing of your own."

Her grip on his hand remained firm. "We've just met, but come with me. Let's see what the next chapter has in store."

He surveyed the camp residents, most of them gathering their belongings, a bedraggled swarm of the unwashed and unwanted permanently migrating over the face of the earth. The halt, the lame, the wounded. The untouchables, the Roma, the bearers of scarlet letters written in the shameful hand of a society that would shake them from its skin given half the chance. He knew he could always rejoin the stream. The decision came suddenly but it felt right.

"OK. I'll go and try it for a few days. But first, come

with me. I need to say a couple goodbyes."

He helped Cindy take down her tent, then pulled the thermoses out of his backpack. He poured out their contents on the ground, then stowed them again alongside his mat and sleeping bag. He carefully rolled his tent and attached it underneath. Then the two of them hoisted their packs and made their way toward Roger underneath the overpass. He was assembling his few earthly possessions, and when he saw them coming, the anger on his face turned to a sad smile.

"It's always the same, isn't it?" he said. "The impermanence of our lives on full display. News at 10:00. City officials with microphones in their faces, blah blah blah."

He reached out to shake Henry's hand, then nodded at Cindy.

"Where will you go?" asked Henry.

"I've been in this city long enough. I think I'll head south. I know San Francisco is crazy these days, but Cindy got me thinking about it, and there are plenty of places to pitch a tent. Want to join me?"

"No," said Henry. "Cindy and I are going to a sort of commune along the Columbia River Gorge."

Roger looked at Henry inquisitively, then turned his eyes to Cindy. "I'm sure this goes without saying, even if you've only spent a few hours with him. This is a good man, Cindy. In a world where too many people think only of themselves, this is a good man."

Roger then moved towards Henry and the two of them embraced.

"Take good care of yourself, brother," said Henry.

"You too, man. Are you going to say goodbye to Arturo?"

"For sure. It's my next stop."

The two of them let go of their embrace, locking eyes for a second and nodding, then Henry turned to Cindy.

"One more place before the bus station."

The camp was now in turmoil, a lot of people shouting their objections, the police restraining themselves. So far, it appeared to Henry that no one had been arrested. They wove their way through the congestion, then walked the three city blocks to the back entrance of St. Francis. Arturo answered after the secret knock.

"Henry and Cindy. What's the matter? Something wrong with the coffee?"

Henry shook his head. "Not at all. The police are rousting the camp."

"Man, what a shame. There must be, what, a couple hundred residents there? And the city knows it's a shell and pea game. Drive the people out of one place and they just go to another pocket of the city."

"Yeah," said Henry, laying down his pack and pulling out the thermoses. "Sorry I poured the coffee, but I want you to have these. Maybe St. Francis can use them. Who knows? Maybe I'll be back sometime to resume my rounds in this area."

"Are you sure?"

"Yes. They're too heavy for the road." He put his hand on Cindy's shoulder. "Cindy knows a place for us to spend some time up in the woods and we're taking the bus there."

Arturo looked at Cindy, then back at Henry, a sad expression etched into the lines around his eyes. "Before you go, I have something for you. I'll be back in a second."

He reentered the kitchen, and the sounds of clanging pots and hissing steam echoed from the interior. A smell emanated from inside that Henry, having eaten hundreds of meals in shelters, had dubbed "industrial strength cuisine."

"I felt this when I first met him," said Cindy. "Arturo seems like such a good guy."

"One of the best I've met."

Arturo returned, holding a small package wrapped in plain brown paper. He handed it to Henry.

"What's this?" Henry asked.

"Open it and find out."

Henry peeled back the wrapping, careful not to rip it. Inside was a bulky envelope with some money and a handwritten note that said, "As you make the rounds in your life, please know that we love you and will pray for you. – the staff at St. Francis."

Henry felt a lump in his throat. "I appreciate this, but couldn't you use the money for something else?"

"It's for you," said Arturo, "a 10% tithe from the alms that we kept aside. We figure you're a good investment. Let yourself receive for once rather than just give. You deserve it."

Arturo sighed. "Tell me again where you're going?"

"Henry is going to join me at a place called Tamanass," said Cindy, "a retreat center in the forest along the Columbia River."

Arturo swept his eyes along the alley, then lifted them to the sky just as a helicopter came into view, the whupping of its blades increasing in volume until it passed directly over them toward Freedom Camp. "Air support for the roust. I hope no one gets hurt."

He stepped fully through the door and he and Henry embraced.

"Namaste, God bless you, as-salamu alaykum," said Arturo.

"Mitakuye oyasin, the Force be with you, keep on truckin'!" said Henry.

They both laughed, released each other, and then Henry turned to Cindy.

"Time for the bus station."

As the image of the two of them receded down the alleyway, Arturo whispered a silent prayer.

"You know I don't really believe in you, St. Christopher, but I know your story. The patron saint of travelers, the one who rescued a child from a raging river. On the outside chance that you're really listening and have some divine influence, keep these two travelers under your watchful care."

Another goodbye, he thought. *Another page turned. Another chapter closed.* Then he sighed again, closed the door, and returned to his duties.

8

Henry and Cindy watched the panoramic beauty of the Columbia River sweep by outside the bus windows. Scattered clouds cast shadows on the blue-gray waters banked by sand bars, pines, scrub oaks, and tall grasses. Henry spotted an osprey in the distance clutching a fish in its talons. He could smell both his own and Cindy's body odors, imagining what it would feel like to take a cleansing bath in the river's current, or even to let its undertow pull him to the darkest depths of the Pacific, where those infamous claws scuttle across the floors of silent seas.

Cindy seemed lost in thought, then suddenly she turned to him. "My mother was always listening to her records when I grew up. She and I would dance to the tunes sometimes. Those are some of my best memories of her. I remember this song called America by Simon and Garfunkel. A man and a woman are on a bus, and they imagine the secret lives behind the faces of different people seated around them. Do you know that one?"

"I do. It's a classic. *She said the man in the gaberdine suit was a spy.*"

"Yes! *I said be careful, his bowtie is really a camera.* Want to play that game?"

"I guess so," said Henry, feeling a bit awkward, reminded again of how long it had been since he'd enjoyed female company or engaged in a playful activity. "But you first."

Cindy chuckled and surveyed the other passengers in the half-full bus. She nodded at a Black teenager sitting a few rows in front of them, dressed neatly, her posture erect.

"She's been living with her family in one of the small towns out here, and she just got accepted to a university. She will go on to be part of a research team that makes a world-changing discovery in cancer treatment."

Henry smiled, drawn to her positivity. He surreptitiously scanned the other passengers, not wanting to make them uncomfortable. His eyes rested on a White man, mid-40s, his face covered in a rough beard, a black watch cap pulled down over his ears.

"That guy looks calm on the exterior, but he's conflicted inside. For about a week now, at a secret spot in the woods near his home, he has witnessed a UFO landing then taking off from a clearing. He's not sure whether to tell anyone because he's afraid they'll think he's crazy. He's been hiding from the craft behind some trees, but he's going to reveal himself tonight. He even has grandiose thoughts that he'll be the one remembered for first contact."

"Doo, doo, doo, doo," sang Cindy, imitating the old *Twilight Zone* tune. "So you want to get bizarre, eh?"

She nodded at an Asian woman near the front of the bus. Middle-aged, she was dressed in what looked like a worker's uniform, her dark hair pulled back in a tight ponytail.

"That woman may also look normal, but she's the keeper of an ancient secret, a Chinese potion passed down through generations that helps a person live forever. Government agents from various countries have been trying to find her for centuries, since she is over 300 years old. She lives with a group that calls themselves the Ancient Ones and their hidden community has been growing steadily."

Henry laughed and nodded. "It's funny how many myths and legends there are about trying to discover a source of eternal life. I never found them appealing. I've enjoyed portions of my life, especially the years with Marsha. But there's also been so much pain that I'm not sure I'd want to live more than my allotment of days."

"Jeez," said Cindy, chiding him. "You and your doom and gloom. Get out of your head and stick with the subject. It's your turn."

Henry nodded at a middle-aged man sitting two seats ahead on the opposite side of the bus. He was dressed in khaki pants, a denim work shirt, tennis shoes, and a safari hat. He was clutching a leather satchel on his lap, his arms wrapped around it like he was afraid someone would try to snatch it.

"That guy lost his wife a couple years ago, and while he was searching on Facebook for names from his past, he discovered an old high school sweetheart. They began messaging each other and he found out that she had also lost her spouse. They began to share at deeper levels until he decided to come visit her at the home she and her husband built in the woods for retirement. In that satchel is a file folder of photos, including one of the two them at their junior prom. He's nervous about meeting her, but he's also excited. He hasn't felt this alive in years."

"I love that," said Cindy. "Second chances are rarer than most people think."

Henry nodded and stretched, exposing the scars on his forearms.

"Can I ask you where you got those?"

He looked down at them, flexing until the welts grew white and stood out like fat worms. He pointed to a cluster on his left arm.

"To be honest, I'm not sure how I got these. I came out of one of my worst blackouts to find myself alone in a stretch of desert outside Las Vegas. My arm was bleeding from these cuts, but I had no idea how I got them. That was a couple months before I got arrested and ordered into treatment. When I saw all that blood, I knew I was crawling across a bottom that was deeper than ever."

"What about the ones on your right arm?"

"I got those from a wire fence, like what happened to the back of your leg. I saw a woman in a Houston encampment being nabbed by a guy against her will. He had her arms pinned behind her and was pushing her quickly forward. I shouted and ran after them, catching up just as the man was trying to drag her through a hole in a chain link fence. I pulled them back and caught my arm on the metal."

"What happened then?"

Henry frowned. "It wasn't pretty. If the guy had been packing a gun, I might not be here. I got the woman free and I messed him up pretty badly. My pent-up rage made me feel like Bruce Banner."

Cindy saw his fists clenching and unclenching at the memory. Once again, she wondered if this man was a human IED waiting to explode. Had she made a mistake inviting him to Tamanass?

Henry noticed her flinching, so he forcibly relaxed himself. "You know what I remember most from that episode? When the woman got free, she didn't say a word. She just walked away down the alley, and before turning onto the street, she looked back at me and nodded slightly. I can still see her face. There's a whole gallery of those images from these past few years. They haunt me sometimes."

Cindy was silent and the two of them continued to enjoy the luminous scenery outside. She pointed out a couple waterfalls visible through windows on the opposite side of the bus. As she had done the night before, she reached over and took his hand, wondering if the anger he had just experienced was still radiating from him. Henry felt her calming warmth spread into his body. He squeezed her fingers gently. The bus took a right turn, and shortly thereafter, Cindy used her other hand to point to a settlement along the highway up ahead.

"That's our stop."

The bus hissed to a halt as the two of them pulled down their backpacks and exited onto the shoulder of the road. There weren't many buildings, but the town clearly had some history preserved in its small main street. A quaint post office caught Henry's attention. "How do we get there from here?"

"We might get lucky hitchhiking, but we'll probably be walking the rest of the way. Let's grab a few things to eat and get some bottled water."

She led him to a rectangular metal building that seemed to be the only source of groceries in town. Near the entrance was a wooden sculpture of Sasquatch, finely crafted, a striking work of art. An array of fresh flowers, two votive candles, and a couple sticks of half-burned incense were strewn around its base. One was still smoldering, releasing the scent of sandalwood.

Henry chuckled. "I wonder what kind of prayer you say to Bigfoot."

Cindy laughed. "Who knows, but if you wanted a spirit to protect you, Sasquatch would kick ass."

The store had premade sandwiches, so they each bought one along with packages of cookies and bottles of water. The woman who worked the counter had gold studs piercings her ears, nose, and eyebrows. A streak of pink dye ran through her hair, and tattoos sleeved her right arm. As they placed their items on the counter, her eyes scanned their dirty clothes and worn backpacks. Undoubtedly, she also smelled their unwashed bodies. Henry recognized Johnny Cash's cover of *Hurt* playing from a speaker overhead. *You can have it all, my empire of dirt...*

"Are you two from around here?" the cashier asked, feigning a smile but clearly not approving of their appearances.

"Yes," said Cindy, her voice tone and body language

disarming the woman's defenses. "We've been gone for a while, but we're headed back to Tamanass."

The woman relaxed, nodding her head and smiling more genuinely. The name Tamanass had some credibility. Henry smiled as he handed her his debit card. *People may look counter-culture on the exterior,* he thought, *but they can still be parochial.*

"Tell Jean hi for me," the woman said. "Tell her it's been too long since we got some fresh vegetables from that amazing garden."

"I will," said Cindy. "What's your name?"

The woman looked guarded again, but then said, "Just tell her that Angie looks forward to seeing her again someday."

"OK, Angie. Will do."

As Cindy and Henry returned to the street, Cash growled I will make you hurt.

"Is Jean an institution around here?" Henry asked as they hit the sidewalk.

"Pretty much. She's been here 20 years."

"I've never lived that long in one place, even when I was a child. My dad had a job that moved us around the country. I wonder how being in a permanent home changes you."

"You'll be able to ask Jean yourself. She doesn't let anyone stay for more than a night without interviewing them personally."

Cindy hoisted her pack. "Let's go. We have a long hike ahead of us."

9

Near the edge of town, they turned right onto a black-topped road that led through the forest. The word that came to Henry's mind was idyllic—late morning sunlight shining in cathedral shafts between tall trees, a stream gurgling through stones on their left. The song of a warbler echoed overhead, reminding Henry of a birding book he once had on his office shelf. He had a sudden longing to put a name to that trill, as if it somehow mattered, an urge he hadn't felt for years.

Cindy hadn't lied about her hiking tempo. Henry had to shift into high gear to keep up with her, but it felt exhilarating to get some exercise and breathe fresh air not laden with city fumes. A few cars and trucks passed them, and though Cindy stuck out her thumb, no one stopped. She slowed her pace slightly, getting into a rhythm that would allow them to comfortably talk.

"You mentioned that your father had a job that relocated the family," she said. "What did he do?

"He was a ranger with the National Park Service. We were stationed at two parks in Utah—Zion and Bryce. Then we moved to Seattle and he worked at Olympic National Park. Finally, he was posted at the Lake Mead National Recreation Area in Nevada. I was a sophomore in high school by then, so I attended the campus in Boulder City. That's how I ended up getting my degrees at UNLV and staying on to teach there."

"I bet it wasn't easy being uprooted that often, but those must have been beautiful places to live."

"They were. Absolutely. And even though my father was the ranger, it was my mother who cultivated my love of the outdoors. She usually held part-time jobs with the companies that ran the park's lodging and concessions. The rest of the time, she took me hiking, fishing, and swimming. Her appreciation for nature was contagious."

He recalled a vivid memory. "We had this small boat when we were stationed at Lake Mead. I remember her taking me out at dawn to go fishing. The striped bass were roiling the surface and as we cast into them we got one strike after another. I'll never forget my mother's laughter echoing out over the water in the early morning sunlight."

"She sounds like a remarkable woman. You didn't mention any siblings."

"Nope. It was just the three of us."

"Are your parents still alive?"

"They are. When my dad retired a few years ago, they moved to a small town in Idaho where both of them can enjoy outdoor activities."

He shook his head and took a deeper breath. "They

were super supportive during Marsha's illness, flying out to be with us near the end. But I feel bad about what's happened since then. When I dropped out, they were understandably worried. They have no idea how far I crashed. I just told them I was on sabbatical, seeing the world, writing and trying to get my head straight after Marsha's death. I set some firm boundaries and asked them to trust me. They've respected that distance, even when my supposed sabbatical extended way beyond a year. I occasionally send them post cards, presenting a pretty picture of my adventures, and I call them every once in a while."

"They must be suspicious after all this time."

He swung his eyes to her. "I'm sure they are. But enough about me. Tell me about your family."

"I was also an only child. We were pretty unremarkable, except that the primary breadwinner was always my mother. She was an elementary school teacher who went on to get a master's degree, then a doctorate in education. She ended up in administration. She was a principal at two different schools, then a superintendent of a large district. She was a driven and capable person."

"What about your father?"

"The word I would use to describe him is kooky. He worked on-and-off at different retail outlets, but he had these other pet projects that occupied most of his time and attention. The longest lasting was his dream of becoming a chocolatier."

"Really?"

"Really," said Cindy with a smile. "He called his little enterprise Miracle Confections. I have to admit, he was talented. He took some classes on chocolate making, and then he made batches of different types of creams. He would box them and sell them at a couple outlets. But the business never took off. I just remember that no matter what he chose to do, my mother always supported him. I appreciated that about her."

"Are they still alive?"

"Very much so. Like you, I don't communicate with them often. Just for different reasons. During Trump's first presidential campaign, they veered hard to the right and embraced all that MAGA bullshit. It surprised me, especially given my mom's intelligence. I'm on the opposite end of the spectrum, so it led to a lot of arguing and emotional distance. They sold their home in Southern California for a huge profit and moved to Tennessee to be in a red state. They intentionally didn't use me as their agent. It was a clear message. Like I said, we don't talk very often. When we do, we try to keep it pleasant. I haven't spoken to them in months. They know about Kevin's attack, but I told them to stay away and let me deal with it on my own."

She suddenly motioned to their left, pointing out a picnic area secluded along the stream. "I've eaten here before. Let's stop and have some lunch."

"Good idea."

They picked their way down a narrow trail to an old wooden table, its surface scarred with decades of carvings. A slight descent in the stream gave birth to a small cascade and Henry marveled at its beauty, sunlight swirling at its base. They took the sandwiches and water out of their packs and began to eat.

"I've wanted to ask you," he said, "what happened in your experiment with ayahuasca that made you want to run away? Are you willing to share that?"

She turned her gaze to the opposite bank of the stream. "It's still pretty fresh."

"If it's too painful, I understand."

She was quiet for a moment as they both listened to the gurgling water. "It was the third time I joined the ceremony. I had eaten a cleansing diet of fruits and vegetables for a few days to prepare myself. As usual, the gathering started with music, and this time, after some nausea, I felt like I was circling around something I couldn't quite see."

She hunched her shoulders. "Then it became clear. I saw myself from a distance, like I was hovering above. I was lying in that hospital bed after the beating from Kevin. I could see my face and arms all bruised, and the doctor had made the incision for a cesarean. She kept exchanging glances with the nurses and all their eyes were full of sorrow. I was crying, both in the image and in the reality of the ceremony. The doctor lifted Sarah out of my womb. Her body was that of an infant, but she had an old woman's face. She looked right at me, opening her mouth as if she was about to speak, as if she wanted to tell me something."

Cindy shook her head. "That's when I screamed and I felt someone's hand resting on my shoulder. It was Jean trying to comfort me, but I shook her off and got to my feet. I was shivering uncontrollably. Jean stood and tried to put her arms around me, but I broke free and stumbled back to my tent. I wrapped myself in my sleeping bag and stayed there until morning. As soon as I got up, I packed my things and left without saying goodbye. I really regret that."

Henry remained silent, giving Cindy a moment to compose herself.

"I didn't mean to cause you any pain."

"It's all right. It's real. It's my life, like it or not. And I'm determined to write a new ending, whatever it takes."

"I'm curious. Do other people have the same kinds of painful trips during ceremonies?"

"Some do. Ayahuasca is known for bringing unhealed trauma to the surface. I read that they're experimenting with it to treat PTSD. But mostly, people have an experience of a greater and more beautiful reality outside their normal lives. I remember one woman in our debriefing circles. She said she was lying on the ground, feeling the earth beneath her and gazing up at the stars. She said she truly understood for the first time that her body is the sacred temple of her soul, and that her consciousness is part of the expanse of a great Spirit or God."

Cindy turned to look Henry in the eyes. "Then she said, 'To me, this realization is the beginning of all wisdom.' Do you hear that depth?"

"I do, and to be honest, that kind of clarity has nibbled at the edges of my awareness when I've been hiking alone in the mountains. But it's fleeting. It always leaves me disappointed. Like it's still wishful thinking rather than any real presence outside of me."

He took a long swig from his water bottle. "Given the pain you experienced, why do you want to return?"

"Tamanass is far more than those monthly ceremonies. It's far more than my little drama. You'll see for yourself if we end up spending any time there."

She took another bite of her sandwich, chewing thoughtfully.

"Besides, I think I'll always regret not hearing what Sarah wanted to say to me. I want to go back and see if I can listen this time. Maybe I'll never get the chance, but I want to try."

"Even if it causes more pain?"

"I think so. We'll see. Anyway, let's get back on the road."

They resumed their hike, and now the sun had risen directly above them, beating on their heads and shoulders. Cindy pushed them with her brisk pace and an hour later they came to a dirt road that veered into the forest on their right.

"This is our turn."

A quarter mile further, they came to another dirt road that branched to the right. A simple but beautiful sign made of highly polished cedar hung on a tree at the crossroads. *Welcome to Tamanass*, it said.

"Here we go," said Cindy, like she was about to cross the border to a foreign land.

10

After the initial rush of finding Cindy, Kevin was at a stalemate. He knew he couldn't approach the home without risking arrest, and it seemed after a few weeks that Cindy's routine would never change. She had hunkered down, and though he occasionally saw her in the backyard speaking to the same woman, he began to check on her less often. A month went by, then two. Instead of slaking his desire to confront her, the waiting made it worse, his need for retribution growing stronger by the day. He wanted to penetrate her smugness until she shouldered her share of responsibility; he wanted to puncture her superiority. The anger was always on slow boil, and anytime he thought of her the heat turned to high.

At his court-mandated classes on anger management, as well as his Gambler's Anonymous meetings, he acted contrite and grateful for the guidance others provided. But the instructor in the anger class, seasoned by years of experience, could sniff out the bullshit of his students. He cornered Kevin after one of the classes.

"When are you going to start getting real?" he asked, his dark eyes penetrating Kevin's veneer.

"I don't know what you mean. I'm participating in the best way I know."

"Yeah, yeah. Keep building that wall of denial. Just realize that you're hurting yourself in the long run. You're shooting yourself in the foot and it's going to cripple you."

Kevin had turned and walked away without another word, seething underneath.

He could tell that his probation officer was equally skeptical, but the man was at the end of his career and jaded. He eyes would scour Kevin's face, then he would sigh and ask a few perfunctory questions. Kevin would produce the sign-in sheets that showed he was complying with attendance at his groups, then make vapid comments about what he was learning, parroting paragraphs from a workbook they handed out to participants. It was a meaningless ritual, neither of them pretending that any real change was happening.

Meanwhile, at work, he had told Steve about what led to his jail time and release, telling a version that cast most of the blame on Cindy. It was due to her mercurial moods and the hormones of pregnancy, he said. He minimized his own violence, claiming self-defense, and he left out the part about losing their baby. He had only hired Steve the previous year, so they weren't that close, and when Steve began to object to the distribution of the workload because of Kevin's absences to attend classes, Kevin said, "Be patient. I'm learning what I need to make better decisions."

But Steve was also street smart. He sniffed out the lie, and Kevin knew that the only reason Steve didn't walk away was that the client base for the business, built up over many years, was still bringing in a good cash flow.

What Steve didn't know was that the entire enterprise was a house of cards. Kevin kept the books, and he had recently secured a line of credit, money he used to pay off his gambling loans and keep the business barely afloat. His obsession with Cindy had kept him from making the usual rounds of card rooms and off-track betting sites, but he knew that if the business had even a few weeks of mediocre activity, he would be unable to make the loan payments. The house of cards would tumble and join the rubbish heap alongside his marriage and foreclosed home.

I'll make it right, he kept telling himself, *but first I need to find her. She needs to take some responsibility for all this. She needs to admit that it is not all my fault.*

One day, almost four months after he had found her, the LoJack app on his phone pinged with a notification. Cindy was on the move, and the address where she stopped was familiar—Vanessa, a friend of Cindy's since college. Cindy and Kevin had double-dated with Vanessa and her husband a few times. Vanessa had recently gone through a divorce, and Kevin had always felt that hanging around her had been a negative influence on Cindy, souring her view of their own marriage.

Kevin had imagined he would spring into action. After all, this was the opportunity he had been waiting for. Instead, he felt restrained. Up until that point, his stalking had been invisible. No one was aware of his locations or intentions. If he crossed this line, he knew that his life in Huntington Beach was over. His business was over. He would be breaching the restraining order, and they would revoke his probation. He also knew that once he got in Cindy's vicinity, he couldn't predict how he would act. Would he lose control again, like the night he attacked her and sent this crazy train speeding on its tracks?

And so, he waited. He kept his eyes on the app and would cruise by Vanessa's house a couple times a week. He thought it was odd that Cindy hadn't driven her car at all, but he figured that Vanessa was chauffeuring her, complicit in her desire to stay hidden.

Two weeks passed. He went to his classes. He checked in with his probation officer. He became more adept at faking his rehab. But inside, the pressure mounted slowly, his obsession with how Cindy had betrayed him. He even saw her contemptuous face leering at him in his dreams, challenging his manhood, his sense of self, his very existence.

Finally, it was too much, and one afternoon, as soon as he could excuse himself from work, he drove to Vanessa's home.

11

Following the sign that led to Tamanass, Henry and Cindy walked a hundred yards further until they came to a tiny home whose porch overlooked the path. A barebacked man with striking looks emerged from its door and came down the steps. He was tall and very brown, his dreadlocks falling over his shoulders. His high cheekbones and aquiline nose set off lustrous dark eyes that spoke of Asian ancestry. A large tattoo of a raven curled around his torso onto his well-muscled chest.

"Cindy!" he exclaimed. "I didn't know if we would ever see you again!"

"Manis! I didn't think I would ever return."

They moved towards each other and embraced with obvious affection. Looking over Cindy's shoulder, Manis locked his inquisitive eyes on Henry.

"Who's your friend?"

"This is Henry. We met in the city at a tent encampment, but the police were driving everyone out, so I invited him to come with me to Tamanass."

Manis nodded thoughtfully, reaching out to shake Henry's hand. He had a strong grip, not overpowering, but full of latent force. "I don't know if Cindy told you our guidelines. Since she vouches for you, we'll allow you to stay overnight. But you'll have to meet with Jean in the morning. She's the one who will decide if you can stay longer."

Manis laughed. "It's just the way it is. You need the Queen's approval."

Henry chuckled. "After hearing such good things about her from Cindy, I look forward to being received in her court."

"Then we're set," said Manis. "Cindy, you know where the platforms are. There are at least two that are open side by side. Set up there like you did last time."

"We will, and maybe we'll see you at dinner."

She motioned to Henry, and they walked further along the road. Henry's first glimpses of Tamanass made him realize that he had broken one of his cardinal rules: don't assume. It was a hard-won truth drilled into him through countless hours spent in the rooms of AA, where he encountered so many people whose appearances and language caused him to make snap judgments, especially in the early years when his ego hadn't been so thoroughly dismantled, when he was still attached to shreds of his academic hubris. Some of the roughest of those characters surprised and inspired him with their wisdom.

He had envisioned Tamanass as a raggedy-ass collection of broken-down trailers interspersed with tents, a slight upgrade from the street, but not much. Instead, he found a quaint village in the middle of the forest, like the setting for a Renaissance fair. Small cabins, tiny homes, and brightly colored yurts lined a series of well-kept pathways that threaded out from a huge central garden ripe with vegetables. The pathways were bordered with flowers and decorative stones that looked hand-painted. There were some older trailers, but even they gleamed with pride of ownership. What also struck Henry was the sheer number of these dwellings, dozens more than he had expected.

Numerous men and women were working in the garden, pulling weeds or gathering vegetables into baskets. As they passed alongside, some of them shouted "Cindy! Good to see you again!" and "We knew you would be back!" Cindy called a few of them by name and waved with obvious affection.

"The prodigal daughter returns," said Henry.

She laughed. "Maybe not that dramatic, but similar."

To their right, a pathway that was wider than the others led to a distant clearing dominated by the largest Quonset hut Henry had ever seen.

"That's the Ark," said Cindy, anticipating his question. "It's a dining room, a gathering place, a space to practice yoga or Tai-Chi, and sometimes a classroom for retreats or seminars. We've had some fascinating guest speakers. Like a Chinook elder who taught some of the ceremonies and traditional medicines of his people. The Ark looks plain on the outside, but you've got to see what they've done to the interior."

Henry nodded. "I'm a bit ashamed to admit that I

expected a lot less when you first mentioned this place. I had these stereotypes of communes or survivalist camps. Maybe even some images from the dystopian novels I've read where people had to hide in forests and scavenge for building materials."

Cindy laughed. "I hear you. When that woman at the shelter first turned me on to the idea of coming here, I had a similar reaction. But Jean runs things like an efficient business. She has an artistic flair that inspires everyone to take pride in being here. Each person has a task and is expected to contribute to the best of their ability. Jean's love for Tamanass is contagious."

She stopped and pointed to a much larger cabin in front of them, the last structure bordering the forest beyond. It was an A-frame, its metal roof a deep green, fronted with an expansive porch where planters sprouted with bursts of vibrant flowers.

"That's the Queen's castle," said Cindy with a snort. "It was the first home on site, and Jean helped build it with her own hands."

Hearing Jean referred to again as "the Queen" raised red flags for Henry. Living on the street had stripped him of so many ingrained attitudes, but never his mistrust of authority. When he occasionally reacquainted himself with national politics or corporate machinations, his wariness of people in power only grew stronger. Thinking of Jean, other stereotypes and assumptions kicked in. Cultic leaders. Authoritarian religious groups. A brave new world in the woods.

"Both you and Manis refer to Jean as the Queen,"

he said. "It sounds sort of medieval. Does she run this place like a feudal kingdom? Does she consider those people working in the garden her serfs? If so, I'm out of here."

"Jeez, overthinker. Relax. The word Queen is like a term of endearment. Jean has her rules and her business methods. She's also strong-willed. But if people present other viewpoints that make sense, she's also flexible. I had some of the same feelings when I first got here. Then I sat in our weekly community meetings and discovered what Tamanass is really like. Each person's input matters, sometimes even newcomers after only a few days."

She took a deep breath of the forest air. "Let me think of a better way to describe Jean. Benevolent dictator doesn't fit because she really doesn't dictate. I would call her Supervising Partner or Primary Facilitator. And there's something about her that makes you want to trust her almost immediately. That trust is important because she also acts as our guide during ceremonies. There's a Spanish word I learned that might describe her better. Curandero. Anyway, you'll meet her tomorrow and get your own impressions. You might have a completely different take on her."

Cindy led him down a trail that branched to their left and they came to some raised wooden platforms about a foot off the ground, the area round them filled with coarse sand. They were surrounded by tall pine trees that still afforded a view of the sky above.

"This is where we can pitch our tents."

They did so, stowing their gear inside, then Cindy suggested they use the communal water station to do some laundry and bathe. It was an area near the tents, fed by a well, with large metal tubs for washing clothes and a couple outdoor showers. Further to their left, in a large clearing that let in ample sunlight, was a cluster of solar panels. Near them were two huge generators.

Cindy reached up and turned on one of the shower spigots.

"You'll soon see that no one is modest around here," she said with a laugh, stripping off her clothes and stepping naked underneath one of the showerheads. Her body was toned, and Henry didn't try to hide the fact that he was drinking in the sight of her. She simply turned to face him completely, smiling as the water streamed down her body, fully aware that he was enjoying the view.

Instead of turning away, he undressed in front of her and stood under the second showerhead. The water was bracing, but the chill felt delicious after their hot and dusty hike. When they had both dried and Henry had changed into his only other set of clothes, they did their laundry the old-fashioned way using scrub boards, hanging the articles on a series of clotheslines nearby.

Henry felt more alive than he had in years.

12

After Manis watched Henry and Cindy walk into the heart of Tamanass, he returned to his tiny home that doubled as a guard shack. He picked up a book he was reading on Native American spirituality, but his mind strayed to memories of Cindy.

Her first time at Tamanass was dramatic. She had a charisma that attracted people to her, and they bonded with her quickly. Manis had expected her to remain in the community, perhaps renting one of the available dwellings. But whatever happened in her final ayahuasca experience unhinged her. He had rarely witnessed such a visceral reaction. He could see her pain and panic when she fled the ceremony and ran to her tent. The next morning, she was gone, and both he and the other residents felt an emptiness at her departure.

Despite how warmly he had just greeted her, his feelings were mixed. He wasn't sure why she had returned, and the guy with her had a strong vibe. His eyes were keenly observant, and his comment about being received into the queen's court hinted at his intelligence. Manis noticed the scars on the man's forearms, wondering what tales they could tell. His intuition was that both Cindy and Henry might be unstable. He had turned on the walkie talkie he and Jean used to communicate, trying to convey his concerns in a neutral tone, especially given Jean's inclination to extend grace. But he was feeling a bit anxious, so he calmed himself, returning to the state of mind he had painstakingly crafted for years. It was one in which he kept his opinions on hold and tried to practice the compassion and hospitality at the core of Tamanass. He knew firsthand that providing a sanctuary for healing was their primary mission.

He remembered how desperately he had needed this nurturing space to get his own bearings. Honestly, he could relate to Cindy having an incident that rocked her world. Just yesterday, for no reason he could trace, the memory of that pivotal night in Berkeley came to mind. Joining the other Antifa members in their black outfits and helmets, busting through the police barricade, shoving into the crowd of alt-right supporters. That moment when his rage exploded on a police officer, slamming the man to the ground and beating him. Finally, having eluded arrest, standing alone on a side street, looking down at his hands and wondering what had become of Manis Johnson.

13

Henry and Cindy spent the rest of the afternoon taking a leisurely tour of Tamanass. Cindy hadn't overstated the renovations done to the inside of the Ark. It was covered in murals, reminding Henry of the famous painted churches he had visited near Schulenburg, Texas. But here, the subject was nature, not baroque depictions of Roman Catholic myths. The corrugation of the walls had been filled so that they were smooth, then painstakingly painted with images of the forest: flowers, trees, mushrooms, a blue stream, deer and squirrels and birds. On the branch of one of the trees was a striking image of a great horned owl, its round eyes peering down on the room. The ceiling was adorned with images of stars and planets. Long tables lined with chairs filled half the room, all of them gleaming with cleanliness. At the far end were large swinging doors that led to an institutional-sized kitchen.

"What an inspiring space," said Henry. "I love the

murals. Who painted them?"

"An artist named Hope. This was her exchange with the community. I hear it took her almost a year. Everyone feels that she gave far more than she received. When I walk in here at any time of day, the beauty just swallows me up."

They passed through a back entrance to another trail that led further into the forest. About 50 yards away, Henry saw a structure that reminded him of a pagoda built from rough-hewn lumber. It somehow fit perfectly into the mood of Tamanass and the surrounding forest.

"This place continues to amaze me."

"We call that building the Portal. Another artisan spent a couple years here, exchanging labor for his stay. I guess he received deep healing through the community and our ceremonies, so he wanted to make this offering. He was not only an excellent carpenter. He also knew how to teach others to assist him. Sort of like a Habitat for Humanity site."

In front of the building was a huge fire pit surrounded by stones where at least two dozen people could sit. Cindy stepped towards the doorway, motioning him to follow. "Let me show you. You have to see it inside to fully appreciate it."

He followed her into a sanctuary that had an oak floor polished to a high luster. At its center was a squat round table, carved with intricate designs that looked totemic. Cushioned mats for sitting were stacked against one wall. Wooden shutters, now open to the outside, revealed huge windows that let in both the light and the lushness of the forest. The roof beams still had their bark, gradually slanting upward to a circular frosted skylight that illuminated the room with a soft glow. The smell of white sage incense was faint but unmistakable, as if it had seeped into the pores of the structure.

"It's astounding," said Henry. "So serene. Is this where you hold the ceremonies?"

"It is. But people can also come here and meditate respectfully. We don't really have this idea of holy space vs. regular space, but Tamanass definitely has reverence for the Portal. Let's hang out for a bit."

She pulled a couple of cushioned mats onto the floor, settled onto one of them, and patted her hand on the other, inviting him to sit. As Henry settled down, he watched her lift her gaze towards the skylight, and he decided to ask a question he had held in reserve.

"So, have you decided to experiment with ayahuasca again?"

She didn't turn to him but spoke into the space above.

"I'm not sure. Part of me wants to find another way. I keep thinking that maybe I can process that first experience with people like Jean or Manis, or even Alma who I hope you get a chance to meet. But another part of me feels like the understanding and healing I need will only come through additional ceremonies."

"Tell me more about Manis," he said. "He has a strong presence.

"His story is amazing. I heard him share it one night in the Ark. He was a radical activist who got involved in one social justice movement after another. Occupy Wall Street.

Black Lives Matter. The protest at Standing Rock. He even spent time with Antifa, which he's not proud of now."

"What do you mean?"

"The way he tells it, Antifa became an excuse for venting his anger. At the time, he felt the anger was justified by the injustices he sees in our society. But he slowly began to realize how much of his rage came from his own background. He grew up in a poor neighborhood of Philadelphia. He had a Black gangster father that he rarely saw, and a Filipino mother who latched on to any man who would support her drug habit. Some of those men were abusive with Manis when he was a kid."

"So what happened? He seems forceful, but he also radiates a sense of calm and clarity. It's almost uncanny."

"He was at the famous Antifa rally in Berkeley in 2017. You remember that one?"

"I do. It was all over the news. They were there to protest the university's hosting of Milo Yiannopolous, the Breitbart guy."

"Exactly. Manis says that during the riot he joined others as they surged into the alt-right crowd. He got into it physically with one of the police, somehow avoiding the officer's club. He threw the officer to the ground, kicking him in the groin repeatedly until the guy vomited on the inside of his riot mask. He said he felt like he was possessed."

"Anger can do that. You and I both know that firsthand."

"True, and for Manis, it was a turning point. The liberal mayor of Berkeley called Antifa a gang rather than a movement. That's when Manis realized that he had become no better than the father he always hated. He said that no matter how he justified it, his violence only caused more violence. He used that famous quote from Gandhi. 'An eye for an eye will only make the whole world blind.'"

"What did he do after that?"

"Sort of like you. He drifted around the country, living at various communes. He worked as a volunteer, including time on the Navajo Nation helping them build water wells. He finally ended up here, and he said that it was like coming home. He's been here many years now, and everyone respects him. I can't think of a single incident when he has been harsh with anyone. That includes a time when a new resident came unglued. The guy was sitting and muttering by himself during a meal. Then he suddenly threw his plate against the wall and started screaming. I thought he was going to attack someone. But Manis went quickly to his side and somehow calmed him down. He didn't raise his voice or make any physical threats. I wish I could have heard the words he spoke. It was like pouring olive oil on boiling water. The guy settled down and Manis took him outside for a long walk in the woods."

"That's a remarkable turnaround for any person. It speaks volumes to the power of this place. No wonder you wanted to come back."

She turned to him with intensity in her eyes. "We've only known each other for a short time. You heard some of my story, some of my pain, but you really don't know the demons I struggle with. I'm not sure you'd be here with me if you did."

He simply shrugged. "I could say the same to you.

I've noticed you looking at my clenched hands when I told you about rescuing that woman. I know you must have a lot of questions and doubts about me. What we've shared so far is just the cliff notes."

She winced.

"I don't just mean about the level of my anger," he quickly added, "but how thoroughly my grief has changed who I am and how I see the world."

Her face relaxed and she nodded thoughtfully. "Then I guess we should get better acquainted."

"I welcome that."

"I think I do also," she said more hesitantly. "Meanwhile, let's go get some dinner."

When they got to the Ark, it was packed with residents. Many of them embraced Cindy and welcomed Henry with the same grace and hospitality shown by Manis. The meal was served buffet style on a table at the end of the room. It was simple—a huge salad of greens from the garden, rice stir-fried with other veggies, and a long pan of sautéed fish. Both of them were famished and ate full helpings of everything.

Afterwards, they retrieved their dried clothing and returned to sit on the platforms in front of their tents. The sun was setting, the nocturnal sounds of the forest becoming more pronounced, like a changing of the guard. Henry found the redolence of the evergreens intoxicating. It brought back so many memories of hiking in alpine settings, mountain peaks silhouetted against twilit skies, lakes like mirrors reflecting the final light of day.

Despite their agreement to get better acquainted,

they sat in a silence that Henry found comfortable, especially after the cacophonous sounds of the city that assailed Freedom Camp, the white noise of human civilization. He began to think about his upcoming session with Jean in the morning, and it reminded him of another pivotal meeting...

2018, University of Nevada, Las Vegas.

"It would be different," said Ramon, "if this was a solitary occurrence. But there have been seven students who smelled alcohol on your breath and saw that you were inebriated during class. They reported it anonymously, of course, and it if were only one or two I might have ignored them. But the sheer number is a corroboration all its own."

Henry was seated at a large wooden desk across from the department head, even now feeling hungover. Protest was futile, so he simply shrugged.

"I have no defense. I know things have gotten out of control."

Ramon looked at him with something akin to compassion, an unlikely response from the often arrogant and erudite professor.

"Listen, Henry. All of us in the department feel empathy for you after Marsha's death. We know what a rare relationship you had. We know you must be suffering tremendous grief. Is there anyone you can talk to and get some help?"

Henry had prepared for this moment and knew exactly what he would say.

"My contract allows me to take a sabbatical given the years I've accrued. I think I want to exercise that option

and try to finish my book on Conrad."

Ramon examined him closely, undoubtedly noticing his flushed face, the sweat on his brow, and his faintly bloodshot eyes.

"If we approve that, will you promise to get some help and arrest this descent?

"I promise."

"OK. I approve it starting immediately. We can have Lydia and Murray cover your remaining classes since there are only a few weeks left in the term. Just email your lesson plans to them."

Henry knew that the approval on the spot meant that Ramon wanted to spare the department and the university any further embarrassment. It rankled him at some level, but he also understood. He got up and Ramon extended his hand.

"Good luck, Henry. I truly mean that. You have a keen mind and a strong spirit. The world needs you."

"I appreciate your help, Ramon. I truly do."

He shook Ramon's hand, and as he turned and walked through the office door, he sensed in his heart that he would never return.

Henry was brought back by the feel of Cindy threading her fingers into his left hand. She had moved closer to him and now leaned her head against his shoulder.

"You went off somewhere again. I've seen you do that a couple other times. And your face had a pained expression. Are you okay? Do you want to share?"

He squeezed her hand a little tighter and let out his

breath.

"I was remembering my last day at the university, sitting in front of the department head with a terrible hangover. I had undermined so many years of study and preparation. Suicide by degrees, one drink at a time."

"But you got sober. Think of that instead. How long now?"

"Almost five years."

"Do you ever get cravings to go back to it?"

"I did in the beginning, but not for a long time."

"I've had other friends who struggled with addiction. Some made it back, a couple didn't. I remember one of them saying that anyone who stays sober is a walking miracle."

She squeezed his hand. "You're a walking miracle."

"Yeah, that's me. Lazarus back from the grave, but the smell and feel of being in the tomb lingers on me every day. I'm afraid I've gotten too used to the odor."

She leaned against him until her lips were brushing his ear.

"You smell just fine to me," she whispered.

Then she kissed him on the cheek.

14

When Kevin got to Vanessa's house, he didn't see Cindy's Honda, but Vanessa's Prius was in the driveway. He strode resolutely up the front walkway and rang the doorbell, aware that someone would be watching through the door cam. He tried to assume a gentle posture and smile. When he got no response, he knocked once, twice, then a third time, insistently growing louder. Finally, he heard a faint shuffling sound on the other side of the door.

"Go away, Kevin," said Vanessa through the speaker. "You shouldn't be here."

Kevin felt his anger pique, trying to keep it from showing on his face.

"I only want to talk to her for a few moments. That's all."

"Just go away. She's not even here."

"Then where is she? I know her car is in your garage."

There were a few seconds of silence on the other side of the door.

"I'm serious," said Vanessa. "Don't make me call the police."

Something snapped inside Kevin. He punched the door, then quickly moved to his right, where a wooden gate secured the backyard. Using his work boot, he splintered the gate, then ran to the back patio. Looking through the sliding glass door, he could see Vanessa talking on her phone. Her eyes were full of fear when they met his. Pumped on adrenaline, he picked up a heavy patio chair and smashed it through the glass.

Vanessa screamed, dropped her phone, and fled to the kitchen with Kevin right behind her. She reached for a knife from a holder on the counter, but he was quick enough to grab her arm before she got hold of it. She wasn't a large woman, so it was easy to pin her arms behind her back and press her face was against the kitchen's marble counter.

"I told you," she spit out. "She's not here."

"Then where is she?"

"I can't tell you. I won't tell you."

While holding her wrists in a vice-like grip with one hand, he used the other to clamp around her throat, focusing his rage into a squeeze that began to make her face turn red.

"Yes, you will."

He eased off his hand and in between choking sounds he heard Vanessa whisper something indistinguishable.

"Speak up. I can't hear you."

With tears running down her cheeks, Vanessa whispered "A place called Tamanass somewhere in Oregon.

I swear that's all I know."

Kevin squeezed her throat again. "If you *ever* tell anyone that you gave me that information, I swear I will return."

That's when Kevin heard two sounds simultaneously. One was Vanessa's cellphone ringing from where she had dropped it on the floor. The other was a police siren in the distance. By the time the officers made it to the house and found Vanessa gasping on the floor, Kevin was in the wind.

15

Jean was a willowy woman, her gray hair hanging in two long braids over her shoulders. Light streamed through the A-frame windows and illuminated her face. She had pronounced crow's feet around her eyes, but the rest of her skin had a glow and texture that contrasted with those wrinkles. She was dressed in an embroidered blouse, a peasant's skirt, and boots made of calfskin.

The front room of her cabin showcased an array of stunning paintings that featured Native American themes. There were totem poles, forest scenes with tribal people walking among plank houses, and two that imagined indigenous women morphing into animals—one into a raven, the other into a wolf. The air smelled of white sage incense.

Jean's intense blue eyes bore into Henry. "Welcome to Tamanass. This place is sacred to me and a lot of other people. But I'm sure Cindy already told you that."

"She did. She also told me that every newcomer

must be interviewed for their suitability."

Jean laughed. "That's true, but if you've spent any time studying human behavior, you know why. I believe that all people are sacred, but not all people choose to actualize their divine identity. Not all people are willing to take responsibility and live productively in a community."

"I've spent a lot of time on the streets," he said, "and that's a fair assessment. Even a few troubled individuals can wreak a lot of havoc."

"Then you know. It's not that we turn away people with troubles. Just the opposite. I consider Tamanass a place where people can find healing and resolution. But again, that takes self-initiative. It takes a willingness to look within. It takes work."

"I found the same thing with my students," he said. "Some of them coasted along, as if the world owed them something, but others took hold of each assignment in a way that furthered their growth. It was always a delight to be around the latter."

"So, you were a teacher. Are you willing to share your background with me? I love a good life story and I love to listen."

Maybe it was because Cindy had already drawn him out, causing him to reveal more than he had to anyone in years. Or perhaps it was Jean's presence, a forthrightness that invited vulnerability. Whatever the reason, he started to unfold the details of his past: growing up in various places around the country, the way he excelled in academics during high school, and his education at UNLV.

After a few moments, he paused, afraid that he'd

be boring her to tears. But she looked at him with the same intense interest and simply nodded her head. So, he continued. Meeting Marsha while she attended the UNLV School of Nursing, their romance, their marriage, the years of beginning their careers in Las Vegas, their attempts to start a family. Then her death, his grief, his drinking, his rehab, the years of roaming through nature preserves and major cities from one coast to another. As he had with Cindy, he recounted the beginnings of his care for those on the street starting with Alex in New Orleans.

To his great surprise, he didn't stop there, even sharing the darker side of his current state of mind, feeling suspended between life and death, suicide and a sense of purpose. It was a torrent of words and he thought, *I'm hardly making myself a suitable member of a new community.* But as they poured out, he had a strange sensation, as if part of him was splitting off to observe himself, a clinical detachment, and there was something his psyche was trying to tell him that he couldn't get hold of.

When he had unburdened himself, he felt sheepish. Exposed. But Jean's face lit up with a beautiful smile. "Has anyone ever told you that you're inspirational?"

The question surprised him. "Not for a long time. And you must be very kind or somewhat myopic to find inspiration in my sordid story."

"The messiness of our lives isn't sordid. It's human. We *all* have wounds we usually hide from others. I've learned that those wounds can become our greatest sources of strength."

"And you have your own?"

"Of course."

"Turnabout is fair play," he said, realizing he was being bold, perhaps rude, but determined to test the water. He had nothing to lose. He could always return to the city. "Are you willing to share them?"

"I am."

She told him of growing up in Los Angeles in a solid middle-class family that never withheld its approval and encouragement, even when she came out as gay in high school. She admitted she was blessed to attend Scripps College due to her parents' savings. She studied public relations, and it was there that she met Rachel, the love of her life. The two of them went on to live together in the hills of Hollywood, opening their first gallery because of their common love of innovative art. Rachel handled the business side while Jean did the scouting and courting of new talents, eventually landing some up-and-coming LA artists that got national recognition. Representing them proved lucrative, so they opened two other galleries on the West Coast, one in Santa Barbara, the other in Santa Cruz.

Jean paused, her smile fading. "It seems ideal to that point, doesn't it?"

"It does. What happened?"

"Rachel grew restless. She never seemed satisfied with what we were doing. I thought it was my fault. I wanted so badly to please her that when she decided to see other women I agreed to an open relationship. But it killed me inside and we drifted further and further apart. Finally, she told me she wanted to liquidate the galleries so that we could go our separate ways."

She looked at Henry with a pained expression. "People speak of amicable divorces. What they usually mean is there were no legal problems that needed to be sorted out in court. Ours was amicable if you use that definition. But if you define it as friendly, I didn't feel that way. I felt stunned and betrayed, then extremely angry, even though the warning signs had been there for years."

"Where is Rachel now?"

"She's living in Chicago. She has a new partner and they've started an online business that sells refurbished paintings and antiques to a high-end clientele. They seem happy. I used to troll their Facebook and Instagram accounts, even after moving up here, but that was masochistic. It only hindered my freedom."

"I'm sorry for your loss."

"Thank you," she said. "And I am for yours."

They looked at each other in silence. Henry hadn't known what to expect, and once again he had committed the error of assumption, imagining there would be some kind of imperious tone to Jean. Instead, he had found a person who was clear, vulnerable, imminently human. His surprise must have shown on his face.

"Are you uncomfortable with this level of sharing?" she asked.

"A bit. But another part of me is relieved. It's just not what I expected."

She laughed. "Ahh, yes. Expectations. I have to tear down their tyranny on a regular basis in my own life."

"How did you end up here?" he asked. "And why the connection with ayahuasca that Cindy has told me about?"

"After the split with Rachel, I was adrift. A friend invited me to visit her in the Sacred Valley of Peru where she was living in community with a group of locals and international expats. I intended to stay for a couple weeks but ended up being there six months. They taught me everything I've transplanted to Tamanass. Their cooperative work style, their communal decision-making, their use of ayahuasca. I was hesitant to try the sacred vine at first, but I found that it truly helped me work through my grief over losing Rachel."

"The Pacific Northwest is a long way from either LA or Peru," Henry said. "Again, why here?"

"Rachel and I had friends in Portland that we visited on numerous occasions. They took us hiking in this area along the Gorge. We loved it, especially me. I kept a lookout for available property and found this 30-acre piece being sold at a reduced price through the liquidation of an estate. I jumped on it. My intent was to use the model I learned in Peru, letting word of mouth spread the news of my experiment through the network of alternative communities. It's been twenty years now and I never dreamed it would grow to this level."

She straightened her shoulders, an obvious shift in gears.

"Anyway. I welcome you again. But if you want to stay for more than a couple days, you'll need to be a productive part of our community. You're also welcome to make a monetary contribution to our operation."

Henry thought of the tithe given to him by St. Francis. "I can do that on both counts. What task do you have for me?"

"It seems you have a gift and a therapeutic need to serve others. Over the years, we've taken in a few residents whose health and age have made it difficult for them to handle daily activities. They aren't quite shut-in, but close. We could use some help from you and Cindy to care for them. How does that sound?"

"It's fine with me if it's OK with Cindy. Let me talk to her and let you know by dinner time."

He stood up from the chair and turned to leave.

"One more thing before you go," said Jean.

He turned to face her.

"Do you know what Tamanass means?"

"Not a clue."

"It's a variation of a Chinook word that means, among other things, spirit guide. I don't romanticize the Chinook. They had slaves and rigid social classes. The elite practiced what I consider a form of mutilation, flattening the heads of their infants between two boards before they were a year old. It was a sign of social status."

She shook her head and shrugged her shoulders. "But still, the idea of a spirit guide speaks deeply to me. I found that presence here at Tamanass. The forest, the community, and the medicine of the vine can all act as guides for people as they take the next step in their evolution."

"And please understand," she continued, "there's no pressure whatsoever to experiment with ayahuasca."

"I'm not one to be pressured into anything," he said, not defensively, but with the firmness and steady eye contact he had developed on the street.

Jean laughed.

"Inspirational and fierce. I like that. I hope you stay for a while. Perhaps you'll find a way to resolve some of your grief, to live with the memory of Marsha in a new way. Perhaps you'll discover that sometimes we *do* need to die, not physically but in the realm of the spirit, before we can find a new fullness."

16

Following Henry's departure, Jean sat on her porch in a splash of morning sunlight. She could see workers tending the garden in the distance, and a soft breeze, perfumed with the scent of pines, played across her cheeks.

She hadn't told Henry the latest chapter in her story. After recently leaving her partner in Chicago, Rachel had called Jean and wondered if they might reconnect. Jean was pleasant with her but maintained a firm boundary. It had taken too many years to resolve that grief, and the time spent with Rachel seemed like a distant incarnation. She'd learned her lessons; it was pointless to return. "No, thank you," she said," surprised with the ease and certainty of her words. "But I wish you all the best." Rachel had been silent on the other end of the call, then simply said goodbye and hung up.

She hoped that Henry could find a similar resolution. His state of mind was ripe for transformation, a phenomenon she had seen many times with pilgrims who arrived at

Tamanass. Though she had no traditional religious beliefs, Jean believed that something—call it Spirit, destiny, or providence—drew people inexorably towards the places and people they needed to actualize their lives. That is, if they were willing to listen and follow. Her role as a spiritual midwife in that metamorphosis continued to fill her with gratitude. It was a calling she had never imagined during her years of managing art galleries. The fact that it was unforeseen only strengthened her belief that every person might be amazed, even stunned, at what life has in store for them.

She thought of her walkie-talkie conversation with Manis the day before. She appreciated his protective caution. He was a balance to her natural openness, and she relied on him in many ways. However, her intuition raised no red flags with Henry. He was clearly hurting, and he had shown a flash of fierceness, but he also displayed a compassion for those living on the edge that mirrored the mission of Tamanass. Maybe he was a kindred spirit. If he stayed any length of time, it would become clear.

When her thoughts turned to Cindy, she was more dubious. She felt a natural kinship with Cindy, but that last evening of her first visit was etched in Jean's memory—the fearful look on her face and the way she had torn free when Jean tried to comfort her. Whatever vision had come to her during the ceremony had rocked her psyche. It made Jean wonder why Cindy would even return.

That persistent force, she thought. *That gravitational pull to learn what we need and overcome every barrier.*

Manis had suggested that Jean interview Cindy

again for her suitability, framing it as a chance to catch up, but Jean had decided to lay back and watch. Her instinct told her that whatever Cindy still needed to find at Tamanass had to be surrounded with grace and the healing space of sanctuary. Pressure might drive her away again. Jean would simply greet her with a loving embrace and welcome her home.

A raven swooped down from the forest and landed on the trail in front of Jean's house. Sunlight caused its black feathers to glow iridescently. It was scratching at something in the dirt. Then it cocked its head, looked right at her, and cawed. She thought of the painting in her living room of the woman shape-shifting into a raven. She thought of the raven tattoo that curled its way across Manis's torso. She thought of both the beauty and power of embracing necessary changes in our lives.

She smiled and nodded at the bird, filled with a sense of Tamanass.

17

After his interview with Jean, Henry found Cindy working in the garden next to a short man dressed in gray khakis held in place by suspenders over his bare torso. He was wearing a gray watch cap, his dark curly hair spilling out from beneath it to his shoulders. His beard was lush, his brown eyes full of merriment. He looked like a diminutive sea captain, perhaps of a yellow submarine. He and Cindy were laughing about something, and the man turned towards Henry, acknowledging his approach with a smile.

"You must be Henry," he said, reaching out to shake a hand. Henry detected a slight accent that was hard to place. "Cindy has said a lot about you."

"That's me. And you are?"

"Trevor. Good to meet you. Cindy and I were just remembering a fun time of frolicking down at the stream."

"It was a perfect day," said Cindy, still chuckling. "There's this deep pool with a rock ledge above it. I'll have to show you. A bunch of us took turns jumping into the water and twisting our bodies into some kind of pose. Everyone else had to guess who or what we were imitating."

Trevor laughed. "I remember when you did Suzy the Riveter."

"Yep," said Cindy, pulling back the sleeve of her T-shirt and imitating the famous WWII poster. "And I remember when you did The Thinker."

"That's me," he said, putting his hand under his chin to mimic Rodin's iconic statue.

"What a great day," she said. "For a few hours, the rest of the world and my troubles seemed light years away."

She turned to Henry. "How did the meeting with Jean go?"

"I didn't know what to expect, and I really enjoyed it. She suggested something that I need to talk to you about, but it can wait until later."

"No, no," said Trevor. "The two of you go ahead and catch up. I need to get this to the pantry."

He picked up a basket laden with squash, tomatoes, and a couple eggplants.

"Until next time, Henry," he said, his eyes twinkling.

"Adieu," said Henry, nodding his head.

Cindy watched him walk away, her eyes filled with merriment. "Trevor is a rare soul. He left his homeland of Wales and has traveled all around the world, meeting people on every continent. He always chooses to see the best in them rather than their faults. I would call him a citizen of the world. Tamanass is blessed to have him, especially during the debriefing times following our nights in the temple."

She turned and searched Henry's eyes. "So, what did Jean suggest?"

"She heard about our assistance to others at Freedom Camp. I guess there are some residents here who could use extra help for various reasons."

"Yes, I know a couple of them, and I can get a full list from Jean. What would we be doing?"

"Not sure. Jean hasn't given me any details. I just told her I would check with you and see if it was okay."

"I think it's perfect. Meanwhile, help me pick some more veggies."

They spent a couple hours working in the garden, collecting produce, hauling it to the pantry in the Ark, and pulling weeds between the furrows. At dinner, Cindy introduced him to a number of other people. Henry remained cordial, but he felt the need to be alone and reflect on the events of the last few days. He excused himself from the table and told Cindy he would see her later.

He returned to the platform that surrounded his tent and sat on the edge, using the last of his phone's charge to listen to *Articulate Silences, Pt. 1* by Stars of the Lid. Amid the spaciousness of the music and the beauty of the forest surrounding the tent, he reviewed his time with Jean. He was amazed at the immediate frankness and vulnerability they had shared within minutes of meeting each other. She was a remarkable woman with the vibe of an old soul. The depth of her presence invited you into her clarity. He admired how she had picked herself up from a devastating loss, discovered a new pathway, then galvanized the courage to actualize her dreams.

3

By contrast, he knew that he had no active dreams, no desire to move on. For so long, he had been avoiding the full truth of this realization, like the seductive depths of denial his drinking had produced. A part of him knew that choosing to live in his self-imposed limbo was selfish, even indulgent, a stubborn way of holding on to the pain surrounding Marsha's death. Even the greenest of counselors would encourage him to let go, to break free from the shackles of his grief.

But he resisted that knowledge, and it was more than denial or stubbornness. His life over the past few years was like an ossified depression, one that no longer dragged him down to drink but was still leaden, embedded in his psyche and his bones. The weight was upon him constantly, and as he had wandered the streets, it was underpinned by the pain, inequity, and conflict he saw every day. The broken shards of humanity that he refused to ignore. The socioeconomic forces that crushed so many people. The systemic evils that stemmed back to the dawn of self-consciousness.

If he were sitting with a fellow professor during his days at the university, sharing a late-night glass of wine, he might have joked and described his state of mind as existential angst on steroids. He might have lifted his glass glibly and said, "It's what fuels my creativity."

But now he knew he was a poser, playing the part of a world-weary intellectual, a man whose wounds could quickly erupt into violence. And all the while, there was something else beckoning to him from the horizon of his consciousness. It was that awareness he had felt sitting alone around campfires at alpine heights, or strolling through mountain meadows as he trailed his hands lightly over the tops of wildflowers. There was something transformative close by, made even closer by the presence of Cindy, and that's when his mule-like obstinance was most evident, because he ignored that voice, that presence, to his own detriment.

With her uncanny intuition, Jean had sensed his predicament when she said, *perhaps you will discover that sometimes we do need to die, not physically but in the realm of the spirit, before we can find a new fullness.*

But how could he let go of his past and all that he was dragging along? How! It was one of those simple solutions that seemed to have a complexity beyond his ken.

Late afternoon sunlight filtered through the trees, and a light breeze caressed his cheeks. *The realm of the spirit,* Jean had said. Those words didn't resonate for him, but the death of a part of him certainly did. He thought back to a colleague of his at the university named Howard. They had grown close, enjoying cups of coffee and levels of intellectual conversation that Henry craved. Howard had eclectic tastes, including an interest in writers who had experimented with psychoactive drugs. It led him to craft a class called *Altered States*, featuring a reading list by Aldous Huxley, Timothy Leary, Alan Watts, Ram Dass, and Carlos Castaneda. Henry had wondered if the department head would approve a course that was so far outside traditional subjects, but he did, and the first semester Howard offered it, there was a waiting list for admission. It had the allure of sensationalism.

Henry read the literature, primarily to have a

foothold in conversations with Howard. He had no urge to experiment with psychedelics, but the insights gained by the writers while under their influence intrigued him, especially their recognition of their essential oneness with the world and other creatures as the boundaries of their egos became more permeable.

"These writers and experimenters understand ego not just by our usual definitions of pride or egotism," said Howard at one of their coffee confabs. "It's more about the ways we define our sense of self, the structures we use to navigate our lives. We get so identified with these false notions of self, these societal and familial blueprints, that we barricade ourselves from a deeper and wider reality."

He had pulled a piece of paper from the front pocket of his shirt and unfolded it.

"I've been carrying around this quote from Ram Dass because I love it. Call it a memento vivere rather than a memento mori. Listen. *Behind everyone's learned behaviors and odd eccentricities lurks a soul, ready to make contact if only coaxed out through a crack in the ego.*"

Howard chuckled, carefully refolded the paper, then returned it snugly to his pocket. "You can laugh at me, Henry, but I'm feeling some cracks developing lately, and the insights seeping through are mind-blowing."

Henry hadn't laughed, not then, not now, especially since Howard's comment merged in the present with Jean's statement and the ethereal tones of the music coming through his earbuds.

Am I destined to die here? he thought. *Have I wandered for so long to finally dissolve this madness in a forest of Cascadia? Will I be able to embrace this death in a way that really releases me? And who could I possibly be on the other side?*

Suddenly, in the distance, he saw Cindy approaching with a bounce in her step. She seemed happy, even buoyant, stepping lightly on the earth. Their eyes met and the smile that broke over her face was radiant, sending a warmth through his body that he hadn't felt in years.

18

Kevin had never experienced himself like this. In both the attack on Cindy and Vanessa, he felt he was watching himself and committing the action at the same time. He thought it would scare him, but he felt only cold and callous. He realized that he no longer cared about what happened to him. His marriage, his business, even his sense of self were burning wreckage along his trail, ignited by his rage, and none of it seemed to matter.

Except for finding Cindy. She was his sole focal point, and though he didn't know what would happen when he found her, he was determined to do so.

After that, he thought, *let the chips fall as they will.*

Upon fleeing Vanessa's house, he had driven to a seedy area of town and parked in a dirt lot behind some mature trees. He had watched too many cop shows over the years, so now he wondered how diligently they would search for him. Certainly, his assault had labeled him as a clear and present danger. Should he ditch his car? Should he be careful about using his credit card? Would they really care that much? How widespread would their vigilance be?

In the end, he decided to use his business debit card one final time to take out $2,000, nearly all that remained in the account. Then he deleted the LoJack app, waited until midnight, and drove to a small gravel lot in an industrial zone, a line of warehouses that were shuttered for the night. He wedged the vehicle into a dark corner and set his phone alarm for 4:00 a.m. He had a go-bag packed for a situation like this. It held a couple changes of clothes, toiletries, water, energy bars, and his Sig Sauer P320 wrapped in a cloth.

When the alarm buzzed him awake, he grabbed the bag, abandoning his truck, and walked along a dark street until he came to an intersection. He then used his Uber app to schedule a ride to the Greyhound bus station.

As he slid into the car, the driver acknowledged him with a nod. "Interesting section of town."

It piqued Kevin's paranoia. Was the guy suspicious of him? "Yeah. I have a workshop around the corner. Time got away from me last night so I slept on a cot. My car's in the shop, so in order to visit a friend in LA, I have to take the bus."

Had he said too much? he wondered. He used a cold tone, intent on shutting down any small talk.

The driver shrugged as he pulled the car into the darkness before dawn.

19

Her name was Alma, her handsome brown face lined with decades of wrinkles, her dark eyes lustrous and intent. As they had walked up the stone-bordered pathway to her small trailer, Cindy told Henry that the older woman had been at Tamanass for years. She had run a small curio shop in San Antonio, specializing in handcrafted items from Central and South America, known for her skills as a curator and importer. She also had a reputation as a psychic, something she didn't advertise, but which nonetheless spread through word of mouth, bringing a wide variety of individuals to seek her guidance. One of them told her about Tamanass, and when her husband died, she made a visit. She decided to stay, and though the intervening years she had become a beloved part of the community. She worked in the kitchen, sharing Mexican recipes from her upbringing, but also practiced psychic sessions with those who sought her wisdom.

Recently, a rapid onset of rheumatoid arthritis had

made it increasingly difficult for her to carry out her daily activities. Henry and Cindy had brought breakfast from the Ark, a mixture of eggs, veggies, and quinoa, along with a thermos of coffee. As the three of them ate together at a small table in the trailer, Alma let her eyes run appraisingly over Henry. She had no qualms about seeming inquisitive. He wondered if that was how she began her psychic sessions, or whether this was another indicator that interpersonal boldness was part of the Tamanass milieu. He returned her probing stare with a smile.

"You've got mileage on you, Henry," she said, "but it seems the miles have given you some depth of character."

Henry laughed. "If you can deduce that with only a glance, you must indeed have a gift. All I can say is that it's good to be in a place where characters are welcome."

Alma laughed. "Amen to that." Then she turned to Cindy with a concerned look on her face.

"I was worried about you, dear. It seemed like you were close to some kind of breakthrough. Then you suddenly left. Was the pain that bad?"

"It was. So much so that I'm not sure why I returned. Mostly to be with you and my other friends here. But also because I know I have unfinished business."

"And now you're open to reaching some kind of resolution," Alma said, a statement of fact rather than a question.

"I am. But I'm also afraid."

Alma reached across the table to put her hand on Cindy's. "I understand. I've felt the same thing when I was close to a pivotal point in my life."

She lifted her coffee cup gingerly, then quickly set it down, wincing and shaking her hand in pain. She squared her shoulders and took a deep sigh. "Have you heard of Dr. Rebecca Ray?"

Cindy shook her head. "No. Why?

"Because I love the courageous path she took in her life. She left behind what wasn't fulfilling and set out into the unknown. I memorized a quote of hers about staying the course when things get difficult. *Sit with it. Sit with it. Sit with it. Even though you want to run. Even though it's heavy and difficult. Even though you're not quite sure of the way through. Healing happens by feeling.*"

"I hear that," said Cindy, a bit defensively. "But she's never walked in my shoes."

Alma simply smiled and nodded. Henry had listened to this interchange with continued admiration at how residents of Tamanass seemed to eschew small talk and get to the nub. He loved it. He had always thought of small talk as the epitome of pissing away your precious time.

Alma looked at him. "Excuse me, Henry. I didn't mean to leave you out of the conversation."

"I enjoy listening as much as talking."

"Have you always been that way?"

"Nope. In another part of my life, another incarnation you might say, I made my living with words. The more erudite and eloquent the better. I was more concerned with speaking than listening."

"What role did you play in that life?"

"I was a professor of English and comparative literature, specializing in English and American novels of the 20th century. It was a huge sampling to survey. Like I say, words, words, words."

"You don't value words as much anymore?"

"It's not that per se. It's just that a lot of fiction seems untested in the real world."

"And you think you have a better insight into what you call the real world?"

"A portion of it." He paused, wondering if she was goading him, then deciding she was sincere. "But a portion that has changed my worldview."

"Tell me about that."

"I've been staying among those who live on the street. I think of it as the nether regions of our society, and most of its occupants are lost and forgotten. These places are like heaps of living midden that need be more fully examined because *every one of us* could learn more about our own humanity and our place in history. Instead, we mostly look away. We can't handle what those levels of poverty, brokenness, crime, and addiction say about our country. What they say about our politicians. What they say about our own choices in the supposed land of the free."

Alma studied him quietly for a few seconds. "You make some valid points. But I think we have a lot to learn from every human being, whether they live on the street or in the comforts of a suburban home. Mystery and sacredness are just below the surface, no matter how hard a veneer we form over the course of our lifetimes. Personally, I try to set down my judgments and just be with people anytime, anywhere."

She gingerly lifted her cup again and took a sip.

"But I'm curious. What are the clearest lessons you've learned from being among the homeless?"

He was silent for a moment, feeling again like he had been chastised. Normally, he would have sprung into a debate, but Alma was clearly not being confrontational, just sharing her own thoughts. Again, that frankness of the Tamanass community that he was growing to love.

"To quote Harry Bosch in Michael Connelly's novels," he replied, "everyone matters or nobody matters. So I guess at a basic level you and I are in agreement."

"I love the Bosch character," she said. "I've read a few of those novels. Always chasing after some form of justice. But more deeply, chasing after a healing of his own psychic wounds. I think that quest is at the core of how we live here at Tamanass."

She took a deep breath and sat up straighter. "Going back to your teaching days, who were some of your favorite writers?"

Henry laughed. "That's like asking parents to choose their favorite child."

Alma smiled. "I'm still interested. I've done a lot of reading over the years."

"Well then, not in chronological order, George Orwell, Harper Lee, Joseph Conrad, Aldous Huxley, F. Scott Fitzgerald, Joseph Heller, John Steinbeck, Ray Bradbury, J.D. Salinger, William Golding, Cormac McCarthy, Ken Kesey, Ernest Hemmingway, William Faulkner, Graham Greene, Toni Morrison, James Lee Burke, Ralph Ellison, E.M Forster. Just to name a few. Like I said, a huge sampling."

"Books by a few of those authors have blessed my life," said Alma. "And with people like Morrison or Ellison, I wouldn't say they were *all* untested in the real world."

Henry smiled, enjoying the intellectual engagement. "Point conceded."

Alma nodded. "Do you miss the classroom?"

He turned his eyes away then looked back. "Occasionally. Sometimes I even wonder if I could work my way back into teaching. But so much has happened, and I left under dark clouds. It's not like I could put 'wandered the face of the earth' as a bullet point on my curriculum vitae for some hiring committee. To make it more complicated, I just disappeared after a supposed sabbatical. I wrote a single cryptic email to my former department head as a resignation. I still remember those words, typed on my phone while I was at a bus station in Mobile, Alabama. *Won't be returning. Sorry. Thanks for all your support. Henry.*"

"That must have been difficult."

"I guess so. But compared to the other emotions and issues I was dealing with at the time, it almost seemed insignificant. It's only lately that the gravity of my journey over the past few years has started to catch up with me."

"What about reading?" asked Alma. "Do you still find time for it?"

Henry pulled out his phone from his pocket. "I download books on this occasionally, one of my few remaining luxuries. Which reminds me. The battery is dead and I notice a plug over there. Would you allow me to recharge?"

"Of course," said Alma, so Henry stood and made

his way to the outlet.

Cindy, meanwhile, had listened to the dialogue between Alma and Henry with fascination. She had not only learned more about Henry's background, but another side of Alma had emerged. She studied Henry's face as he sat back down at the table, remembering the nakedness of their bodies and the vulnerability of their glances as they looked at each other while showering. She felt drawn to him, something she hadn't experienced for many years, including in her marriage to Kevin. Again, it was unsettling, but also exciting.

After spending more time with Alma, they made their rounds, visiting the names on Jean's list. Cindy knew a few of them already. There was Peter, a man whose unhealthy lifestyle before Tamanass had severely aggravated his diabetes, leading to the amputation of his lower right leg and the replacement with a prosthetic. He was a nice enough fellow, but also proud and usually unwilling to accept support. His work exchange at Tamanass was to polish the floors of both the Ark and the Portal on a regular basis. Cindy saw how quickly Henry moved through Peter's defenses and got him to admit that he needed help with painting his tiny home, especially using a stepladder. He had already purchased the supplies, so Henry agreed to come back later in the week.

Next they visited Rose, a young woman who was busy adjusting to her firstborn child named Heather. The girl's father was living at another commune on the East Coast, unwilling to provide assistance. Henry and Cindy arranged to give Rose some childcare in a few days so she could run errands in town.

Finally, there was Susan. Her situation was unique. She had arrived at Tamanass six months prior and had been functioning as part of the community by working regularly in the garden. Then, suddenly, she holed herself up in her little trailer, rarely speaking to anyone, simply coming out to eat at the Ark, then returning. Lately, she had even given up that practice, leading a few concerned members of the community to deliver meals to her. Jean had asked them to try and speak with her and figure out if there was a different way forward.

Cindy stopped at the footpath leading to Susan's small cabin and turned to Henry. "Let me see if she'll let me in. I know her a bit from working in the garden. Maybe she'll talk with me. I'll catch up with you at the tents or meet you at dinner depending on how long this takes. All right?"

"Sure."

He watched as Cindy knocked on Susan's door, waited, then knocked again, until finally it opened a crack and Henry could see the two of them conversing. After a few moments, Susan let Cindy cross the threshold and the door closed.

Henry returned to his tent and sat in front of it. Above, visible through the clearing in the trees, dark clouds were gathering. The wind that heralded the storm was already swaying the crowns of the trees, and he could smell moisture gathering in the air. Thunder growled in the distance.

The image of Susan letting Cindy inside her home

spoke volumes to him. Likewise, he had let her come across the entrance into his own life, breaching the emotional distance he had guarded while assisting others in the tent cities. Roger and Arturo were exceptions, but even with them he had never exposed his deeper struggles. Cindy had drawn him out of himself so quickly, something he now realized he had needed, even if it made him feel a bit raw and agitated.

How long has it been since I acknowledged my need for anyone? he thought.

That thread led back to Marsha. One of the things he loved about their relationship was a time every evening when they would sit on the back patio of their home and have a glass of wine, reflecting on the events of their days. Normally, Henry was one who wanted people to get to the point, to gloss over all the details and give him the short version. State your thesis clearly was his motto, a symptom of his aversion to small talk. But with Marsha, he wanted to hear every detail. He just loved being in her presence, something he was now beginning to feel with Cindy.

He thought back to when he first introduced Marsha to his parents, about a year before their marriage. They had scheduled dinner at a fancy restaurant on the Las Vegas Strip. Henry had been nervous, feeling a bit sheepish about his need for parental approval, but his misgivings were unfounded. Marsha charmed his mother and father immediately, and he once again marveled at her grace.

The storm broke overhead, dumping large drops of rain that splattered on the ground and his skin, so he retreated to his tent. He sat listening to water stream off its surface, thunder exploding from above. Suddenly, he heard a voice above the din.

"Hey! Let me in."

He quickly unzipped the tent flap and Cindy squeezed through, her clothing damp from the deluge. She took a seat next to him on his sleeping bag.

"Wow!" she said. "That came up quickly."

Henry pulled his only towel from his backpack in the corner of the tent and handed it to her. She wiped her face, her hair, and then made a pass along her T-shirt and pants. Her nipples showed through the wetness of her shirt.

"How did it go with Susan?" he asked.

"Better than I expected. It turns out she has a history of agoraphobia which she never told anyone about. She expected it to go away by leaving the city and living in the country. At first it did, but then it came back."

"That's such a hard disorder to live with. It can make your world so small, and now even smaller since she's living in a tiny cabin."

"True, but here's the interesting thing. It's not being around the other people at Tamanass that's causing her fear. It's the open spaces around us. The forest, the clearings, the night sky. It's the raw presence of nature. She never thought that would happen, but there it is."

"Where did you leave it with her?"

"She agreed to join me on some hikes into the woods. Just short distances at first. Maybe having a supportive companion will help her get over it."

"I hope so."

They sat in comfortable silence for a few moments,

rain sluicing off the tent. Henry felt Cindy nuzzle up tighter to him.

"The next ayahuasca ceremony is this Friday night," she said. "I've been thinking about it a lot, going back and forth in my mind, but I've decided I'm going to partake and see where it leads me."

"Are you sure?"

"Not really, but it's like Alma said. There's some unfinished business here and I need to sit with it."

"I understand, but I'm not interested in joining the ceremony. My sobriety is dear to me. I'm afraid that any kind of altered state might crack the dam and let that disease flood back over me again."

"I hear you. But there's a way you could participate without sampling the vine. You remember that huge firepit outside the Portal?"

He nodded.

"We keep a bonfire going on the night of the ceremony. A man named AJ has been the firekeeper for years, but he left a couple weeks ago on a cross-country trip to visit his brother. Would you be willing to take his place?"

"That could work. I've kindled a lot of fires during my years of camping."

"Okay. I'll talk to Jean about it and let you know."

A gust of wind swayed the tent and Cindy pressed closer to him. He put his arm around her and pulled her even closer. She turned her mouth towards his ear.

"You feel so good," she said.

He raised his hand to push a strand of hair from her forehead, their eyes looking deeply into each other's. Then, as naturally as taking his next breath, Henry bent his head and pressed his lips to hers in a long and languid kiss. They drank in each other's presence for quite a while, and then she pulled back, nuzzling her head on his shoulder. They stayed like that until the storm passed.

Afterwards, lying awake in her tent after midnight, Cindy felt deeply conflicted. Her mind roamed over the years of her life, especially the early days of her relationship to Kevin. She had never really been in love with him. She knew that now. She had chosen him as a buffer against other boys she had dated in high school. Most of them, even those who tried to hide their motives, were ultimately interested in pressing her to have sex. A couple of her girlfriends had relationships with guys who respected their boundaries, simply enjoying the companionship, but she hadn't been as lucky. Except for Kevin. He was the son of her parents' oldest friends, an easy alternative who wasn't very popular, not the best looking, and definitely not demanding of her physically. She could have chosen to eliminate dating completely, but there was peer pressure, even a cultural imperative, to find someone for romantic engagement. She had gay friends, but she knew she was straight, which narrowed the field considerably.

And so, she and Kevin spent more and more time together in their senior year of high school, staying in touch after she moved away and started attending San Diego State University. By then, she had ambivalent feelings about him. She hoped that being away from him would make their relationship too difficult to maintain. But Kevin started driving to see her regularly. Then they found an apartment near the campus and moved in together. He also enrolled at the school but jumped track to a technical college to get his HVAC certification, a field where his uncle had succeeded.

She remembered his proposal to her. They had been at her parents' home, enjoying a barbecue on the back patio. Cindy's mom, never one to hold her tongue, spoke to them both.

"Since you've been together so long, and now you're living together, why don't you just go ahead and get married?"

Kevin was silent, but he nodded his head.

"That's a big step, Mom," Cindy had said. "We're in no rush. Let us get used to this first."

Cindy's mom laughed in a scoffing way. "Your father and I are still getting used to each other. That's the nature of marriage. You commit and then you commit again and again. I don't see how a short time in the same apartment at your age is going to teach you that."

Cindy started to object but her mother interrupted.

"Look," she said, raising her hand in a gesture to shut Cindy down. "I don't want to argue. You're adults. I just think you seem right for each other and should go ahead and tie the knot."

Later that evening, Cindy and Kevin were sitting alone in the backyard.

"I think your mom is right," he said. "Why don't we go ahead and get married? I think we make a good team."

It wasn't romantic. It wasn't even emotional. But as Cindy heard those words, there was a subtle shift, a sort of acquiescence in her as she nodded, smiled, and said "okay," reaching out to take Kevin's hand. Looking back, she saw how she had chosen comfort rather than adventure. She had settled, and settling was one of the major flaws in her personality. It had held her back for too many years. It was the reason she had fallen into selling real estate rather than starting her own business. It was like living out the scripts others had written rather than choosing her own.

Her thoughts turned to Henry, especially how he had described his relationship with Marsha. The depth of his grief showed her that something else was possible, a level of passionate love she had dreamed about in her youth. Henry had found a soul mate, someone to share his life with at far deeper levels than Cindy had ever known. She had come to wonder if that kind of romance was just a myth conjured by Hollywood and romance novelists. It certainly didn't apply to her marriage, or to the friends in her social circles. Everyone seemed to be getting by, cruising along without passion, choosing creature comforts and busy careers rather than deeper intimacy.

I'm tired of settling, she thought as sleep finally overcame her.

20

It was 8:00 p.m. on Friday night. The flames of the ceremonial fire danced high into the night sky, fed by cords of wood stacked nearby. Henry poked the logs and added new fuel when necessary. It felt good to have a purpose.

Soft guitar music floated through the open door of the Portal, played by a resident named Oscar. Occasionally, voices would accompany the notes—not really a chant, but more like a spontaneous outbreak of harmony. Henry could hear Jean's voice, her words too far away and muffled for him to make any sense of them.

As he watched sparks leap like crazed fireflies into the night, he thought about his moments with Cindy in the tent during last night's storm. After their first kiss, he clearly got the body language that she wanted to slow down. It was fine with him; their sudden relationship had been moving quickly. Neither of them needed to say these things; they were just understood as they held each other lightly. It was like the intuition he had shared with Marsha, and it drew him even closer to Cindy.

A particularly loud pop released an arc of light against the night, and Henry saw another fire forever burned in his memory…

2017, Nevada.

He added a log to the metal firepit. They had rented a small cabin at a resort on Mt. Charleston northwest of Las Vegas. It was a romantic getaway, a chance to decompress from their busy schedules. They were on their second glass of wine, and even then, Henry was already thinking about a third glass from the second bottle they had brought along. Marsha had recently made a few comments about his increased tolerance, but he assured her there was no problem, the wall of denial being built one brick at a time.

"Let's play a game," Marsha suddenly said.

"What do you have in mind?"

"Imagine that these sparks going up into the night are chances for us to let go of something. We have to name what it is that we want to release."

"All right," he said with a chuckle. "You go first."

She nodded; her face suddenly intent in the firelight. She didn't speak for a couple moments.

"I want to let go of my impatience with people at work. When I got into administration, I promised myself I would never forget the human side of why I chose nursing in the first place. But now, the pressure to run my unit like a business has made me cranky and sometimes even callous with my staff. I don't want to be like that. I want to let it

go."

She took a deep breath, lifted her hands to the night sky in a gesture of surrender, then turned to him.

"Now you."

Henry drew a blank at first, but then something formed in his thoughts.

"I want to let go of my doubts about spirituality, about God, about any notion that there is a personal presence greater than us. I don't mean being religious. I just feel that my mind has been closed to any knowledge or experience of things I can't prove intellectually. I want to let go of that."

Following her example, he took a deep breath and raised his own hands in surrender.

They played a couple more rounds that were more humorous, and then they went to bed. Marsha had insisted that they not open the second bottle of wine, so Henry was clear-headed for their slow and passionate lovemaking. Afterwards, they spooned their naked bodies against each other.

"I know there's one thing I never want to let go of," he whispered in her ear. *"And that's you."*

She sighed and pressed her backside even tighter into him.

"Thank you for tending the fire," said a female voice, snapping him back from his reverie.

It was Yasmin, a younger resident of Tamanass that Cindy had introduced him to in the garden a couple days prior. She was looking at him with a smile that brought the word beatific to mind.

"My pleasure," he replied.

Yasmin sat and stared into the fire, retaining her lustrous smile. Other residents began to drift out of the Portal to sit in the ring that surrounded the blaze. Henry didn't want to seem like he was prying, so he furtively scanned their faces in the flickering light. Some had glazed looks in their eyes, others were scrunching their foreheads in obvious concentration, and a few were whispering words to themselves that he couldn't hear. He noticed Manis lying on his back a stone's throw from the circle. Another young man was crying, steadily and openly, unashamed of his emotional display.

Then he saw Cindy emerge. She walked slowly and sat down in the large circle to Henry's right. At first, she didn't acknowledge him, but when she turned to meet his eyes, her expression was almost eerie, reminding him of the girl who had stared at him with old-soul eyes in that Las Vegas alley, an image that had haunted him ever since. Then, as Cindy continued to look at him, her expression took on a fierce quality. She averted her gaze from him and turned back to the fire.

21

For the next two days, Henry and Cindy made the rounds of the list Jean had given them. Henry helped Peter paint the exterior of his cabin while Cindy took a walk in the forest with Susan. They also delivered food to Alma and spent the afternoon caring for Caleb, Rose's newborn son, while Rose took a shopping trip to the nearest village.

Cindy had been cordial but distant. The only time she flashed her radiant smile was when she was cuddling Caleb against her chest.

"Are you willing to share what happened?" he asked after they had gotten Caleb down for a nap.

She looked at him, studying his face.

"Not yet. Maybe at the debriefing."

That debriefing, as Henry discovered, was a communal meeting always scheduled on the third day after a ceremony. The idea was to give people enough time to catch up on their sleep and review their experiences with the sacred vine. It took place in the Portal, with cushions and mats arranged in a circle. Henry had asked Cindy if he was welcome to attend since he had only banked the fire and not imbibed the ayahuasca.

"Of course, and you can even share if you want to. This is an open community, one of the things I love about it."

At the appointed time, a large group of residents gathered in a circle, seated on the many cushions. Henry recognized some of the faces he had seen in the light of the bonfire, and others he had met at dinner in the Ark or while working in the garden.

Jean opened the meeting with a song, accompanied by Oscar who had provided the musical backdrop for the ceremony. It was a simple chant, and Henry soon picked up the words.

Our wisdom awakens. Our memory returns. Within these open hearts, a sacred fire burns. And the Way is simple. The Way is clear. The Way is humble. The Way is here.

When they had sung the piece a few times, Jean let a pregnant silence descend over the group. People breathed deeply, gathering their attention to be as fully present as possible. Finally, one woman broke the silence.

"I'm Jen," she said. "I've met most of you, and you might have heard me speak in our last meeting before I encountered Mother Ayahuasca. If so, you know I was pretty full of myself."

She smiled and Henry noticed a few others in the circle smile and nod as well, conceding her appraisal of herself but not in a judgmental way.

"I now understand clearly that we *all* have our blind spots," Jen continued. "Including me. I've traveled to places like Tamanass all over the planet. I've done what I considered a lot of spiritual work, some of it with the chemical assistance of mushrooms. I considered myself pretty enlightened. I figured that a ceremony here would just confirm what I've already learned about our own divine natures, maybe in a more vivid way."

She shook her head, tears beginning to streak her cheeks.

"Jean told us to have an intention for the ceremony but not an expectation," she continued. "My intention was to discover anything within me that was a blockage to experiencing my fullest self. At least I had enough foresight to realize I might not be as far along as I thought. At least I was willing to challenge my ego."

Her tears were stronger now, as were the compassionate smiles of others in the group. Once again, Henry felt the unique warmth of Tamanass and its communal bonds, so different from anything he had known on the street or in the halls of academia.

Jen wiped her cheeks. "After drinking the tea, I laid back on my mat and listened to the music. But I felt tense, like I was stuck in limbo. I thought to myself, 'is this all it's going to be?' And then I had waves of nausea, something flowing out of me, not physical, but like a psychic vomiting.

"I was crying, and during that I began to see the faces of my extended family on both sides. My parents, grandparents, uncles, aunts, and cousins. And what I felt was the pain that so many of them carried in their lives.

They have passed it on from one generation to another, and that pain was inside me as well.

"Then I saw my mother *so clearly*. She and I have been estranged for many years because her affair with another man is what broke up my parents' marriage. I blamed her. I always have. I've gotten counseling about that. I even wrote her a letter recently, and I felt I had some peace about all of it. But in the vision, I knew I was still filled with judgment and unforgiveness."

She sat up straighter, stretching her arms above her head. "As my mother walked towards me, I remembered so many times in my childhood when she had comforted me while I was sick or after I had fallen down. As she got closer, her face turned into that of another, much older woman, and I knew I was looking at Mother Ayahuasca. She reached out and put her hand on my shoulder and I couldn't stop crying. That's when her face turned into Jean's and I realized that Jean was sitting next to me, wrapping her arms around me while I sobbed, and I let her embrace me in a hug like I've never felt before."

Jen turned towards Jean, clasped her hands together, and made a small bow. "Thank you so much. I see now that what I needed was to be embraced by Pachamama. I needed to start letting go of my own pain and my ancestor's pains at deeper levels. This work needs to continue, but it feels so good."

She stopped talking and wiped the remaining tears from her cheeks.

"Thanks to all of you for listening. Thanks for helping me through this humbling time."

The group, many of whom had cried with her, simply nodded, some of them murmuring, "We love you, Jen."

Oscar began to slowly strum his guitar, softly at first, then gaining in volume as the group sang the same song, and this time the lyrics seemed weightier to Henry.

Our wisdom awakens. Our memory returns. Within these open hearts, a sacred fire burns. And the Way is simple. The Way is clear. The Way is humble. The Way is here.

When the chant died down, Manis began to speak, and a sort of reverential silence fell over the group. Since their initial meeting at the guard shack, Henry had heard many people speak glowingly about Manis. He was the primary male leader in the community, not in a patriarchal way, but through the assumption of a role that others conferred upon him with mutual respect.

"Since we have a few new people to the community," he said, "my name is Manis, and at this point, except for Jean, I've lived at Tamanass the longest. One of the things that continues to amaze me is that my journeys with the vine are still teaching me ways to be a more actualized human being. And I wouldn't want to take these new steps at any other place than Tamanass. For me and so many others, this is truly a spiritual oasis."

He looked around the circle with a warm smile. "In our last debriefing, I shared how Mother Ayahuasca showed me that judging people *in any way whatsoever* causes spiritual sickness. The same goes for our self-judgments, which I struggled with for many years. Negative thinking is a cancer, and my last journey showed me that I needed to expel it more permanently from my body, mind, and soul."

He took a deep breath, then exhaled. "One of the values we have at Tamanass is that being human is a divine gift from the Creator, and so we honor each other's holiness. We also know that every part of the earth is sacred. I've been doing a lot of reading about indigenous cultures around the world. I'm drawn to their animism, the belief that animals, plants, and even the elements themselves speak to us if we're ready to listen. It's a knowledge that we share here at Tamanass. But maybe reading about it in more depth prompted this experience I will never forget."

He rotated his head, stretching his muscular shoulders and neck. "Some of my times with vine have been hard. The insights were harsh and difficult to accept. This one had what I would call a luminous beauty. I was lying on the ground near the firepit, staring up at the stars. I could hear Oscar's beautiful strumming and what I thought was the whispering of some of you around the fire. But then I realized that the whispering was a myriad of voices from the forest, the air, and the stars above me. The whispers gathered into the sound of wind blowing over me and I felt my body literally growing into the ground, as if I was taking root into the mycelial network, the woodwide web all around us. And the stars…how can I even describe them? It was like they were dancing."

His usually expressive eyes grew even brighter. "I felt a sense of oneness with the cosmos and yet I didn't feel that I had dissolved into it. I remained Manis, a joyous part of the sacred temple in which we exist. My own consciousness is part of this mystery people have called God, Spirit, Creator, and it was this very force that was looking out beside me through my eyes. It was a partnership, not an intrusion. It was the deepest feeling of love I have ever experienced."

His face lit up with a joyous smile, and then he laughed in such a contagious way that many in the group joined him. Even Henry began to chuckle and he thought of a quote from Herman Hesse's *Steppenwolf*, one of the few non-English novels he had taught at the university. He used it as a writing prompt for his students, asking them to give their interpretations, so he remembered every word. Like Manis's statement, it was a summation of Harry Haller's quest, and perhaps the soul of Hesse himself.

For the first time I understood Goethe's laughter, the laughter of the immortals. It was a laughter without an object. It was simply light and lucidity. It was that which is left over when a true man has passed through all the sufferings, vices, mistakes, passions, and misunderstandings of men and got through to eternity and the world of space. And eternity was nothing else than the redemption of time, its return to innocence, so to speak, and its transformation again to space.

Lost in that reverie, he heard the sound of Cindy's voice as she began to speak.

"I just want to say something first," she started. "I'm so grateful for the way all of you have welcomed me back. For the hospitality you've shown since I returned. Thank you for embracing me, not judging me. I know I left suddenly without any meaningful goodbyes. There was just so much pain I was dealing with, and it seemed to be more than I could bear. That's been my pattern throughout my life. To run when it gets too much. And I've always felt that

I needed to justify my actions to other people. I have too often looked for approval and acceptance. I haven't listened to my deepest longings as a woman. Right now, I am what I am. That's all I'm going to say about my first time here. Just…thank you."

She took a few breaths and looked around the circle, finding warm and gracious smiles. "I prepared myself for Friday night by accepting that the trauma of losing my baby Sarah was something I still hadn't dealt with."

Alma was sitting in the circle, and Cindy turned her glance to the older woman. "Thank you, Alma. I'm sure you know why."

Alma dipped her head. "I love you. We all do."

Cindy smiled and continued. "I know my grief is still fairly fresh and that it will take its own course. But there's something else there. Something I needed to sit with. Something about my life in general. Some information I needed to understand. Does that sound strange?"

"Not at all," someone murmured, and others nodded their assent.

Cindy also nodded. "I didn't know if I would even get the chance to revisit what I really needed. But Mother Ayahuasca is wise beyond measure, and after a period of restlessness and nausea, I had this vivid image of walking into the forest. It looked like the one that surrounds Tamanass, but denser. There were colorful mushrooms along the path, and ferns and vines coiling around the tree trunks."

She shook her shoulders as if a sudden chill had overcome her.

"That's when the mood shifted. I sensed that something was following me. I looked behind me and all I could see was a huge shadow that dissolved as soon as I focused on it. But it was definitely getting closer, so I began to run, faster and faster, and then it was as if that shadow placed its cold hand on my shoulder, trying to pull me back. But I broke free and suddenly found myself in a clearing in the forest."

Cindy's breathing had been speeding up, showing her agitation, so she slowly calmed herself while others patiently waited. "It's hard to describe that clearing. It was like a cathedral of trees. It seemed natural but also like someone had carefully crafted it. I was no longer being followed. And that's when I saw her, sitting on a huge stone at one end of the clearing."

She reached her hand to cover her mouth, barely suppressing the gasp she emitted.

"My God! How could a human face be so strange and so beautiful at the same time? I knew it was Sarah. She was old. She was young. She was mother. She was my child. She was beautiful. She was haunting. Then, as she looked directly at me, she motioned with one hand for me to come closer."

Cindy grew preternaturally quiet, her eyes taking on that look Henry had seen when she came out of the Portal to sit at the bonfire. Her silence lasted a long, full moment and, to their credit, no one interrupted. They let the quietude grow pregnant, as if creating an opportunity for a birthing as one body, one community.

Finally, Cindy spoke. "Sarah said something to me,

and I don't mean to be hold back, especially since the rest of you are so vulnerable. But my intuition has told me it's a message I should live with in silence for a while. Something I need to think about more deeply before I share it with anyone else. *If* I share it with anyone else. I hope you'll understand."

"The choice to disclose *anything* in this sacred circle is entirely up to you," said Jean. "When you're ready, we're here. Or if you never revisit this story again with us, our feelings for you won't change one bit. You are beloved."

A woman named Emily, who was seated to Cindy's right, lifted her arm and rested her hand on Cindy's shoulder. Cindy turned to her and they fell into a warm embrace.

There were other stories, and the emotional variety and intensity stirred new levels of awareness inside Henry. As the group began to disperse and go back to their chores, he approached Jean who had stayed until everyone left.

"I've had a lot of experiences in my life," he said, "but I don't think I've ever lived through something quite this intense. How do you remain at the center of it and still keep such grace and calmness?"

"Because I approach every debriefing not just as a teacher or guide, but as a student. I know there are things that happen in these circles that are meant to further my own evolution as well. You probably had that experience when you taught at the university."

"Yes. In my better moments, when I dropped the pretensions of being a professor and just entered into dialogue with the students. Those times were always fulfilling."

"If you could consider yourself a student for a moment, what did you learn from this morning?"

"It confirmed something I have known for a long time. Something I have been unwilling to face squarely. There's a new awareness, a new revelation, nibbling at the edge of my consciousness. Something that wants to awaken me. It's been there for a while, but has grown exponentially stronger since I arrived here. Does that make sense?"

"Absolutely. It has happened times in my own life, and I have seen it happen with so many people here at Tamanass over the years."

Henry nodded. "But listening to all this confirmed something else. I don't want to experiment with any mood-altering chemicals, natural or not. It's a part of my sobriety. I don't expect others here to fully understand."

"But I do understand," said Jean. "I understand that this is your truth."

Henry looked away, then returned his eyes to meet Jean's. "Anyone who knows me can clearly see that I need to resolve my grief about Marsha's death and the path I've taken since then. I'm not even sure what that resolution means. It's like that rocking back and forth on the cliff that I told you about. Something needs to give, and I've been putting it off for way too long."

She studied him for a moment. "Meet me at my house at 4:00 p.m. There's a place I want to show you."

"I'll be there."

When he showed up at the appointed time, Jean was sitting on her porch. She got to her feet and beckoned him with her right hand.

"Follow me," she said, leading him down the front steps and towards a tree with a red metal circle pounded into its bark at shoulder height. Next to it, barely visible to the naked eye, was a lightly trodden pathway leading into the forest.

Jean's hiking pace was on par with Cindy's, so brisk that Henry had to put a skip in his step to keep up with her. The trail wasn't long, maybe 200 yards, and then it suddenly ended in a clearing that immediately reminded Henry of the one Cindy had described during the debriefing. It was an almost perfect oval of green grass surrounded by tall trees. In its center was a wooden Adirondack chair with a large flat-topped stone next to it that served as a table. On that table was a small wooden totem, brightly painted, depicting faces of animals and people indigenous to the Northwest.

"I discovered this place while surveying the land before I purchased it," said Jean. "The previous owners must have carved it out as retreat space for meditation. It has become very special to me. I'm usually not protective about anything at Tamanass. Just this clearing. It's a private place that I have used for my own meditation times throughout the years. I have brought many riddles with me here. Many disturbing emotions that demanded some clarity. Even some victories and joys I needed to celebrate more fully. The rest of the residents respect the privacy of this place."

She looked around the clearing with a broad smile, then lifted her arms to the sky. "I've had some liberating insights here. It has become a place of Tamanass, of spirit guidance. providing a deeper link with creation and with myself."

She swept one of her hands in an expansive gesture.

"I don't quite know why, but my intuition strongly advised me to share this sanctuary with you. I welcome you to come here and sit with the questions you have about your own journey, especially your memories of Marsha. If you were inclined to join us in ceremonies, I would have suggested the same focus for your preparation."

Henry was touched, not only by the beauty of this refuge in the forest, but by Jean's generosity and trust in sharing it with him.

"Try out the chair," she said. "See how it feels."

He walked across the carpeted surface of grass and settled into it, realizing that it was tilted just enough to afford a view not only of the beauty of the trees, but the sky above. He heard birds fluttering in the tree branches and the sharp pungency of conifers was intoxicating.

"I don't know what to say, Jean. I'm deeply grateful."

He turned his head to look at her, but she was gone.

22

Kevin felt the pressure of his Sig Sauer P320 against his lower back where he had tucked it in his pants. He had a permit, but no permission for concealed carry. Nevertheless, with his paranoia getting stronger by the day, it gave him a sense of security and power. He knew it was crazy, but he imagined how he might draw it if he was cornered. He thought constantly about the warrant for his arrest following his attack on Vanessa. How far reaching would it be? He had no idea. But the last remnants of his old life in Huntington Beach were a heap of smoldering ashes. He was a fugitive, plain and simple.

He was seated in a dive bar on Motel Street in Fresno, a downtown area notorious for prostitution and drug trafficking. He had paid less than a hundred dollars for three nights in a hotel so seedy that even the roaches seemed to have forsaken it. There were clearly squatters in other rooms on the three floors, their doors and windows barricaded by wood, the remaining stucco on the outside walls coming off in large chunks. The management didn't seem to have the will or inclination to evict them. When Kevin mentioned it, the jaded man at the counter said, "Take it or leave it." Kevin took it.

He looked at his reflection in the mirror behind the bar. He had let his beard and hair grow long. He wore a ball cap, rounding out his new look with a pair of black-framed glasses. He had no idea if the disguise would confuse facial recognition software. He had no idea if that was even something to worry about. He only knew that he was going to be exceedingly careful until he reached Cindy's destination. He had decided to break up his bus trips into short segments, staying for a couple days in the worst sections of various cities up the central part of the West Coast.

The bartender, a middle-aged man with a ZZ Top beard, made his way over.

"Want another?"

"Yeah. One more. Thanks."

The man deftly retrieved Kevin's glass, refilled it with a double shot of Jim Beam, then slipped it across the counter.

"That'll be $10."

Kevin slid $12 to the man, who nodded and moved to the other end of the bar. Spending money on alcohol probably wasn't wise, Kevin thought, but at this point he didn't care if he ran out of his remaining funds. They only needed to get him as far as the Columbia River Gorge. It hadn't been hard to find the commune called Tamanass on the internet. It was mentioned in the comments of many people who had visited there, most of them saying that they found the place welcoming and helpful.

He took another sip of his bourbon. Whatever showdown happened when he caught up with Cindy would be a final episode for him, for her, maybe for both of them. Of that he was certain. He was so lost in thought that he hadn't noticed the woman who sidled into the barstool next to him.

"You seem pretty gloomy this evening."

Her voice was rough, and a smell of cigarettes and booze poured off her body. When he turned to look at her, he saw the heavy makeup meant to hide her age and possibly the last days of her ability to turn tricks.

"I'm just tired," he said.

"Buy me a drink and afterwards I'll see if I can make you feel better."

She lifted an eyebrow and twisted her lips into a half smile, half leer. There was something about the look that reminded him of Cindy's condescending expression in the months leading up to their violent fight. He felt an instant mixture of anger and repulsion.

"Leave me the fuck alone," he grumbled.

The woman recoiled from the intensity in his voice, but she didn't back down.

"You don't have to be an asshole!" she spit out.

He felt the urge to stand up and shove her, but he saw the bartender approaching in his peripheral vision.

"Is there a problem here?"

Kevin lifted both his hands in a gesture of surrender. "No, just a misunderstanding."

The woman had already retreated to the other side of the room, wanting no part of anything that might happen. Kevin stood, chugged the last of his drink, then turned and left the bar. Back on the street, he felt a bit unsteady from four shots combined with the wear and tear of the road. Like a stranger not only to the others that passed him on the sidewalk, but to himself as well, he stood in the wan glow of the streetlights. A final night in Fresno, then Sacramento, Redding, Eugene, and finally the end of it all.

An unexpected memory came to mind. The day of his wedding to Cindy, a small ceremony in a church in Huntington Beach that her parents attended. It wasn't an elaborate affair, just a handful of family members and friends. He saw Cindy coming down the aisle with her father, then standing across from him with the pastor between them. The look in her eyes was flat, her smile controlled, which at the time he had passed off to the nervousness of a bride on her big day.

Did I miss the signs even then?, he wondered. *Was she ever really in love with me, or did she just tolerate me?*

His anger began to simmer again, so he pulled down the bill of his cap and started back towards the broken-down motel.

23

In the days after the debriefing session, Henry and Cindy fell into a rhythm of performing the chores that Jean assigned. Henry did odd jobs for a couple residents, Cindy continued her walks with Susan, and both of them provided childcare respite for Rose. They also ran errands for the community, driving a truck into town to purchase supplies for the kitchen.

Since sharing in the debriefing circle, Cindy's mood was erratic. At times she was affectionate with Henry, reaching out to hold his hand, and then just as suddenly she would drift away, lost in her inner landscape.

"Are you all right?" he asked during one of those quiet moods.

"I think so. I'm still sorting things out."

"Just let me know if you want to talk any further about it."

"Thanks," she replied, reaching over and squeezing his hand.

Henry had confided in Cindy about Jean opening her forest grotto to him. They both agreed that he should only go there alone, honoring Jean's wishes, and he had been doing so in the late afternoon after chores, enjoying the last sunlight before it was eclipsed by the trees.

On one of those occasions, sitting in the Adirondack chair, he felt a light breeze on his cheek. He had always believed that people create miracles because they need to confirm their sense of the supernatural. They see the Virgin Mary in a piece of toast, claim healing properties in springs of water, or place their hands on the tombs of interred saints to absorb the blessings they crave.

They also endow certain locations with a sense of holiness. He didn't deny the appeal of what others called thin places, locales where the supposed veil between earth and heaven was more permeable. He had been to a few of them and their beauty was inspiring, even breathtaking. But it always seemed to him that the litmus test for an authentic spiritual life would be that it cast a redemptive glow on any place you found yourself, no matter how wretched it might seem by the standards of society. He had experienced this firsthand in AA meetings around the country. So often, even in cramped rooms, trailers, or urban basements, there was a transcendent feeling as people opened their lives to each other. If a god, spirit, or higher power really existed, certainly its ability to heal and sustain wasn't confined to rarefied places that only a select handful of sojourners could afford to visit.

Still, he could see why this sanctuary in the forest was special to Jean. Its beauty awakened his senses to a higher state of alert. He looked up at the sky to see a few tattered clouds sailing overhead. Then he closed his eyes, letting the chronic tension in his body dissipate, and a precious recollection of Marsha filled his mind...

2018, 30 miles offshore.

Marsha sat next to him, her back pressed against his chest as they watched the passing whitecaps of the Pacific Ocean. They were on a charter boat circling Catalina Island off the California coast. It was a romantic adventure they had planned long before Marsha's cancer diagnosis and the onset of her chemotherapy. She had finished her first two regimens and she insisted that they still get away on the trip, something her doctor encouraged.

Her hair had fallen out, her head wrapped in a brightly colored scarf that one of her friends had sewn for her. The reds and golds of the cloth contrasted sharply with the pallor of her face, and as he studied the paleness of her cheek, Henry felt a great fissure opening up inside him, releasing a wave of sadness.

"Look!" exclaimed Marsha, pointing off the bow of the boat.

A pod of dolphins was gliding nearby, dorsal fins glistening in the sunlight as they breached the surface, like a pattern of blue-gray waves unto themselves, luxuriously at home in the sea. The sweet tang of ocean brine was like a beckoning, an invitation to dive, to let go, to merge. Henry drew a deep lungful.

"So beautiful, so graceful," she said.

He kissed her behind the ear.

"I want you to promise me something," she said.

"What's that?"

"When I'm gone..."

"Don't talk like that," he interrupted her. "You have..."

"Just listen," she said with a stern tone.

She took a deep breath then continued.

"I know you, Henry. You are hopelessly monogamous. Having a companion in your life is essential. So, when I'm gone, please promise me you will find a way to move on and begin a new relationship."

"I haven't given up hope."

"This is not about hope. This is about a pernicious form of cancer that has spread more quickly than anyone predicted. Honestly, I'm not even sure I would have submitted to the chemotherapy except for your constant urging. Do you understand that?"

"Yes."

"Then I'm serious. I'm asking you one more time because I love you and I know you love me. After I'm gone, will you promise to move on and be open to the possibility of a new relationship?"

The sadness inside Henry welled up even stronger. He pulled her closer to him and whispered in her ear.

"Even though every fiber inside me is rebelling, I promise."

A peal of thunder in the distance brought him back to the moment. Images from the years since Marsha's death swarmed over him. The alcohol tearing away his body, mind, and spirit. The endless, vacant promises to himself that he would quit, that he would start over the next morning, only to give in once again to the cravings. His time in the rehab unit, bonding with an unlikely cast of bottom dwellers like himself. The beginning of his wandering. The mountains, the parks, the rivers and meadows, then the panoply of cities and their homeless encampments. So many faces of all colors and ages, most of them marked with the pain of what had driven them to that station in their lives.

Tears began to run down his cheek, rivulets as alien to his skin as rain on a parched desert floor. And then he began to cry more freely, more forcefully, until he was sobbing, his body racked with a release from cisterns of grief. He lost track of time, not knowing how long he let this inner torrent flow out of him. He only knew that by the end of it, he felt spent. He opened his eyes and drew a deep breath.

"I promise," he whispered to the trees and the sky above.

That evening, after a dinner of mixed greens and grilled fish in the Ark, Henry and Cindy returned to sit outside their tents.

"Now it's my turn to ask," she said. "You seem unusually quiet. Are you okay?"

"I think so. And I've been wondering. Would you be willing to grab our sleeping bags and spend the night in that clearing that Jean shared with me?"

She studied his face, then a smile slowly spread across her own.

"I would love to. You think it would all right with

her?"

"I do. And if it isn't, I'll take the hit."

They rolled up their sleeping bags, put a ground cloth and some water in Henry's pack, then made their way to the clearing. Near the Adirondack chair was a level area of soft grass where they spread out and got settled.

"It's so serene here," said Cindy, resting on her back and looking up as the sky morphed into twilight.

Henry laid down next to her. "I know you don't want to share the fullness of what happened during the last ceremony, but I want to share something with you."

"Please do."

"Earlier today I remembered a moment during Marsha's last days. Even though she was weak from her chemotherapy, we took a trip to Catalina Island. We had planned it a year prior, long before we knew of her diagnosis."

"I love that place."

"I do too, and we had perfect weather. We visited the Wrigley Memorial and Botanic Garden and walked around Avalon Harbor. We even took a charter boat that circled the island."

"So this was a positive memory?"

"Most of it, yes. But while we were cruising, she said something that still stings."

He grew silent and Cindy didn't say anything. He appreciated her sensitivity.

"She was sitting next to me as we watched the passing ocean and she asked me to promise her something. She knew in her bones that she wouldn't survive, something

I was still choosing to deny."

He was silent again, and this time Cindy spoke softly. "What did she ask you to promise?"

"That when she was gone, I would move on and be open to the possibility of a new relationship."

When he said the words, he felt his chest starting to spasm again, so he let it pass. "Being here at Tamanass has sharpened my understandings. It's amazing how quickly it has happened. I guess that when the student is ready, the teacher appears."

He looked up at the twilit sky. "I've become more aware of just how stubbornly I've held on to my grief, thinking it somehow honored the memories of Marsha. But it's a lie. I haven't honored her. I've just humored my ego and pride. I haven't kept my promise to her, and today I saw even more clearly how self-indulgent I've been. I sat in that chair and cried for I don't know how long."

He felt raw and vulnerable, as if someone had used sandpaper on his skin.

"You're so hard on yourself," said Cindy. "I saw that in you the moment I met you. There was this heaviness hanging on your shoulders despite the fact that you were choosing to do some good. Don't get me wrong. I'm not judging you. I've gone through enough of my own depression to understand what it's like."

He turned his head to look at her. "I guess meeting you and coming here to Tamanass has stirred all of this up in a way that demands some resolution. I can't avoid it any longer. A part of me is open to choosing a new way of life for the first time in years, but it also scares me. Where will that path lead?"

She reached over and threaded her right hand into his left one.

"I really appreciate your honesty and vulnerability. I'm not used to that in a man. I've been in such a passionless marriage for so many years that I began to forget what it was I really desired. Or maybe I didn't think I deserved it."

She took a deep breath.

"Since you've been so honest with me, let me tell you the rest of what happened to me during the ceremony."

He squeezed her hand tighter.

"When that vision of Sarah came to me and I moved closer, I had to lean so far toward her that my ear was nearly touching her lips. It was so eerie that it made me shiver."

Cindy moved closer to Henry, tucking up against him. "Then she whispered the oddest thing. She said, *'Mother, child, listen to the wildness of your womb. Only you can decide your future.'*"

"That is odd," said Henry. "It's like the message from an oracle. Now that you've had a few days to ponder it, what do you think it means?"

"At first, the idea of listening to my womb after losing a six-month-old baby seemed way too painful. Then I realized that since she called me child as well as mother, she was helping me reflect on the course of my life. Like she was helping me let go of the past and prepare for the next chapter in my life."

She released his hand and wiped a strand of hair from her forehead. "Lately, I've seen so clearly how I've stuffed my own desires over the years. My own wildness. It's too early to make any long-range plans. But I know that deep inside me—in my womb if you want to put it that way—I want to experience the woman I was created to be. And there's something else. I still want to have a child if the right situation and relationship arises. Even the death of Sarah hasn't destroyed that longing. And there's a defiant edge to all of these insights. I won't let Kevin's violence put a permanent end to any of my dreams. It would be like letting him violate me all over again."

She rubbed her forehead. "The vision given to me the other night is about birthing a new and freer version of myself. There's a wilder and more powerful spirit within me that needs to be released. If that includes another child in the future, it will happen at just the right time."

Henry nodded. "Your words may be different from mine, but I have felt the same urge for release in my time here at Tamanass. And when it comes to a child, Marsha and I tried for years to get pregnant. When it didn't happen naturally we turned to hormonal therapy, intrauterine insemination, in vitro fertilization. Nothing worked. Finally, the stress and the expense were too much. I had resigned myself to never having children, but then Marsha suggested adoption. I was surprised at how quickly I warmed to the idea. We were looking at adoption agencies when she was diagnosed with the cancer."

Neither of them spoke for a while, and their breathing seemed to synchronize. The forest trees were losing their definition in the deepening twilight, and the first stars of night emerged. The temperature began to drop, so Cindy pulled a blanket over them.

Suddenly, a great horned owl, powerful predator of the night, began to hoot from a nearby tree—perhaps steeling itself for a nocturnal kill—then went silent. They continued to lie in that silence until the sky was aglow in starlight, so bright that that it illuminated the clearing without the moon. Having recently spent so much time in the city, the sight was a tonic to Henry, resonating with all the hours he had spent outdoors with his parents, with Marsha, and alone during those first years of wandering.

He felt Cindy reach over and use her right hand to travel up his chest to his chin. She gently pulled his face towards her and kissed him, at first lightly, then firmer, probing his mouth with her tongue. He returned the exploration, careful not to let too many years of pent-up energy overwhelm his response. She gently pushed him to his back and moved her body smoothly to sit on top of him, straddling his hips and unbuttoning his shirt.

"Are you sure?" he said. "I…"

"Shhhh…"

He let her unbutton his shirt and lay his chest bare. Then she bent down to run her tongue from his belly button to his neck, then reversed her motion and moved lower down his body, unzipping his pants and pulling them down, taking him into her mouth, slowly making him harder.

She sat upright and pulled off her shirt, revealing her firm breasts. He cupped them in his hands and she gave a short sigh. She stripped of her own pants, pulled his down until they were free of his legs, then mounted him, taking him fully inside her.

She began to sway forwards and backwards, not rushing her enjoyment, and he felt the union with her as a wave of both pleasure and healing relief. Her motions grew stronger, building to her own rhythm. She threw back her hair with a shake of her head, her face framed against the beauty of the night sky. He made no effort to control the movement, simply letting her be the guide.

Finally, like a wave from within, he came deep inside her, and a few seconds later she followed with her own climax, letting out a short cry at its peak. As her body slowed, she looked down and locked her eyes on his, her expression unreadable. Then she placed her chest against his and encircled her arms around him. They stayed locked in that embrace for a while until they both turned and she spooned against him. Neither of them spoke as they listened to their mutual breathing and the nocturnal sounds of the forest.

Long after midnight, Henry awoke on his back with Cindy breathing quietly next to him. The sharpness of the night sky seemed even brighter, impossibly dense with stars, planets, nebulas, and galaxies far beyond our own. The constellation Scorpius was clearly visible, spreading out against the Milky Way, slowly rotating southward. Every time he absorbed himself in the depths of the heavens, the sweep of history became palpable. These were the same stars under which tribes like the Chinooks had pitched their camps and settlements, the lights that had bathed massive herds of bison moving like dark oceans across the continent. The same stars that had slowly circled above the Continental

Divide with its snowy peaks, and the Grand Canyon as the Colorado River inexorably etched its formation over millennia. The same sky that inspired thinkers, writers, poets, and artists who allowed themselves to be swept up in its beauty.

His mind strayed to another writing prompt he had used to inspire his students during a lecture, words from the Persian poet Rumi. *That's how you came here, like a star without a name. Move across the night sky with those anonymous lights.*

So often during his camping adventures, he had felt another emotion alongside his awe when lying under the firmament. It was the opposite of what Manis described during the debriefing. Instead of a oneness with the cosmos, Henry felt his own insignificance in the face of eternity. Not just anonymity as part of the human herd and its superficial evaluations, but a wave of meaninglessness, the same dizzying darkness that had gripped him as he leaned over that gorge near Mt. Charleston, or atop the overpass in Freedom Camp.

But now, in this moment, the vastness spoke of a different reality. It aligned with the words Manis had shared, as if he, too—Henry Thornwood—was part of this miraculous presence in a personal, vital way, as if the very stuff of stars was swirling inside him, giving testimony to the meaning of not just the cosmos, but his own unique existence. It was a buoyant sense of belonging, even greater than the love he had shared with Marsha, and it flooded through him like a transfusion of joy and hope.

Cindy's breathing caught for a moment, then resumed

its sonorous rhythm. He wondered what dreamscapes she was wandering through, hoping in a protective way that she was experiencing beauty and harmony. The release he had felt with her remained with him, but he also wondered what this meant for their relationship that had developed at such a whirlwind pace. She had seemed so free during their lovemaking, almost in her own world. What would she be like in the morning? Where would they go from here?

He took a deep breath, relaxing at levels he hadn't known in years, completely unraveling that part of him that was steeled and vigilant on the streets. A primal sense of peace descended upon him, a peace that passed his understanding, circumventing his intellect to settle in the recesses of his soul.

He took another long, deep breath, then let go, releasing something elemental inside him, letting go like a sweet experience of dying or crossing over.

24

Kevin walked into the small general store in the roadside village near Tamanass. Angie, the woman who had waited upon Henry and Cindy, was at the cash register. He tried to remain calm, but he felt the tension in his body growing stronger as he got closer to Cindy's location. He placed a small package of cookies and a bottle of Gatorade on the counter.

"I'm wondering," he said, "if you can tell me how to get to Tamanass."

Angie looked at him with the same appraising glance she had used on Henry and Cindy. Dressed simply in jeans, boots, and a Dickies work shirt, he was a tall, well-built man with longish blond hair and a beard covering his face. His blue eyes returned her scrutiny with a hint of defiance. She didn't like the vibe she got from him. There was something off, something hinky, like he was hiding something. As a counter-culture outlier, she was accustomed to unique people who found their way to the commune in the woods.

But this man was out of sync in a different way. Her friends told her she had a raging intuition, and this time her Spidey Sense sent an alarm.

"You have business there?" she asked, making no attempt to hide her skepticism.

And there it was, just as she expected. Something flashed in his eyes, a barely hidden rage, and she watched him quickly struggle to get hold of himself.

"Not really business. A longtime friend of mine sent me a postcard and invited me to visit."

As he said this, his eyes looked down for a second, which Angie saw as a clear indication of lying.

"I'm sorry," she said. "The people at Tamanass are pretty private and don't like me giving out directions. I'm surprised your friend didn't tell you."

She saw one of his fists clench, and then his eyes narrowed, confirming even more that she had sniffed out his subterfuge. A tinge of red crept into the skin of his neck, and she half-expected him to come across the counter at her. She took a half step back, aware of his physical power. Her eyes darted to the front window, hoping that another customer would enter and buffer the tension.

"That doesn't seem very neighborly," said Kevin.

Angie felt her own anger rising. She returned his glare with defiance.

"Well, we *aren't* neighbors. Sorry I can't help you. Maybe try contacting your friend. Some people still have cell service at Tamanass."

The two of them stared at each other for a few seconds, neither one backing off, until Kevin forced himself to cool down.

"What do I owe you?"

She rang up his items, gave him change for a twenty, then watched him turn and walk out the door, its old-timey bell jingling. For a moment, she thought about digging out the contact she had for Jean, a cell phone number she hadn't used for ages out of respect for privacy, but in the end she let it go.

Back on the street, Kevin got control of his breathing. *Fucking bitch*, he thought to himself. He quickly walked to his right along the sidewalk so that she couldn't track him through the store window. About a half block later, he saw the sign for the post office and figured he might have better luck there.

The town seemed sleepy on the exterior, but the post office was bustling, a long line of residents holding packages and envelopes, serviced by a lone employee who was obviously harried.

Kevin got in line with the others, trying to seem as natural as them. He shuffled his feet a bit and checked his watch, mimicking impatience. A middle-aged woman with gray hair immediately in front of him kept sighing, irked by the wait. After a couple minutes, as casually as he could, he spoke to her.

"I'm on my way in from the city. I'm here to pick up a package and deliver it to a friend at Tamanass, but I've never been there before. Her directions were sort of vague. Can you tell me how to get there?"

She huffed and barely glanced over her shoulder. "It's easy. Just take a right at the end of town, go about five miles to the first dirt road on your right, take that and you'll see a small sign for Tamanass and another dirt road. You can't miss it."

She huffed again.

"That is, if you ever get out of here."

"You know what," said Kevin. "I'm going to come back later and see if the line has dwindled."

He slipped out the front door and immediately headed towards the edge of town. Just as the woman had said, there was a sharp turn to the right revealing a road that stretched into the distance. It was bordered by tall conifers, and a stream dappled with sunlight ran along its left edge, murmuring softly. He took a deep breath and launched into the final leg of his journey, tightening the cinches on his backpack.

As he kept a brisk pace, he thought back over the trail that had led him here. He knew it was crazy. In the few Gambler's Anonymous meetings he had attended, they said there was little defense against the insanity of addiction or the personality traits it produces. That had certainly been true when he continued to chase the dragon with his betting. It was the hallmark of an addict, gamblers said, and it could wreak havoc even during abstinence if you were not actively applying the truths of a Twelve Step program.

Kevin had tried working with a sponsor, but the man was hard on him and it only stirred his anger. His thoughts shifted to his broken relationship with Cindy and the financial mess of his business. He felt like he was driving full speed into the setting sun, intent on a crash and burn, but the only thing that mattered to him was some kind of reckoning with the woman he still considered his wife. He blamed her for so much of what had happened.

Too late to turn back now, he thought.

In the initial stage of his journey up the coast, he still had his cellphone with him, but then he got paranoid that it might be tracked, so he smashed it, ditching it in a trashcan at a rest stop between Redding and Eugene. He then bought a cheap burner, and outside a convenience store in Redding, he called Steve one final time.

"What the fuck," said Steve immediately, casting aside any politeness. "Where the hell are you? The police were here at the office a few weeks ago looking for you and I told them I had no idea."

"I can't tell you. But everything is over at this point."

"What do you mean, it's over? I put up bail for you, man. All the accounts for the business are dried up and now you just split? I know we don't see eye to eye, but I've given a lot to this business. And this is your thanks? Hanging me out to dry?"

Kevin had felt the final barrier of his descent crack like an old wooden floor in a shotgun shack. "You can have it all. The equipment, the trucks, everything. Use it for your own business or just sell it to make us square. But it's over. I'm done."

There was a silence on the other end.

"You're fucking crazy," said Steve as he abruptly hung up.

Kevin had felt nothing as the line went dead. His conscience was so seared that the dissolution of his business—all the blood, sweat, and tears expended over a decade—was like a distant occurrence.

Now, after hiking for what he felt was at least five miles in the warm sunlight, he finally saw the first dirt road on his right. He immediately grew cautious. Who would he encounter first? Would Cindy still be here? Would his long journey be a complete waste of time?

He walked another hundred yards until he saw the lacquered sign, then walked for another short distance until he came to tiny home. Immediately, a tall muscular man with bronze skin and a prominent tattoo of a raven on his bare chest, emerged from inside and came down the steps. He stared at Kevin—not welcoming, not hostile—just neutral, his eyes alert.

"Can I help you?"

"I hope so," said Kevin, trying to sound cheerful and relaxed, even as his heart began to thrum in his chest. "I'm here to see a friend named Cindy. Last time I heard from her, she had made her way up here."

At the mention of Cindy's name, Manis felt instantly protective. He knew most of the details about what had originally led her to Tamanass. This had to be the man she had fled, and he wasn't about to let anything happen to her. On the other hand, Jean had instructed him to always err on the side of hospitality. *Who knows what providence brings people to us*, she said. *We don't want to be a roadblock to their healing.*

"We try to welcome everyone," said Manis, "but we also require verification from one of our community members." Manis shrugged his shoulders. "I'm sure you understand. There's only so much room on this property."

"I totally understand," said Kevin, feeling like his heart was going to come out of his throat.

"How about this?" said Manis. "We do have a woman here named Cindy. I don't know for sure if she's the one you're looking for. Why don't you come with me and we'll find her?"

"Sounds perfect."

"By the way, my name is Manis."

"Josh," said Kevin, shaking the hand that Manis offered.

Manis swept his arm towards the road that led into the community and Kevin fell in step beside him. He hoped that the tenseness in his body and his quick breathing weren't too obvious. The gun was still tucked into his pants. His eyes scanned the well-maintained cabins, trailers, and yurts of the community, all of them displaying a pride of ownership. He hadn't known what to expect and he was impressed.

On his end, Manis had registered Kevin's stress. He heard it in his voice, saw it in the rigidity of his body, felt it in the clammy touch of his palm when they shook. It put him on high alert, and he hoped he wasn't making a mistake. He could only remember a few times when he had turned someone away at the guard shack, and maybe this should have been one of them. He wasn't afraid for himself, completely self-confident that he could protect himself. It was Cindy's welfare that concerned him, and he was primed to act if the situation called for it.

They circled the huge communal garden where numbers of people were at work. Some of them looked up with curiosity.

"This way," Manis said, leading Kevin along a dirt path towards two tents pitched on platforms.

That's when Kevin saw her, and it took his breath away. She was hanging clothing on a line strung between two trees. She turned and looked at him, her eyes instantly ablaze with both anger and fear, none of which was lost on Manis.

"No!" she shouted. "You're not welcome here! You're not welcome anywhere in my life!"

As soon as she said this, another man emerged from behind the tents. Kevin took in his strong presence, his steady eyes, his scarred forearms. The man gently reached up to put his hand on Cindy's shoulder, trying to calm her.

"Is it Kevin?"

"Yes," she hissed.

When Manis saw the look on Cindy's face and heard the alarm in her voice, he circled to the left until both he, Cindy, and Henry were facing Kevin.

"So, it's Kevin," said Manis, "not Josh. I don't like being lied to."

"I don't give a fuck what you like or don't like," snapped Kevin, dropping any pretense of civility. "This is my wife and I have a right to talk to her."

Both Henry and Manis took a step towards Kevin, holding their hands at their sides, but showing in their united presence and the steeliness of their eyes that they would deal with whatever Kevin did.

"You may still be legally married," said Henry. "But Cindy just made it abundantly clear that she doesn't want you around her anymore."

"Is that right? And who are you? What gives you the right to protect her or speak for her?

"What gives me the right," said Henry, still calm and sharp as a blade, "is not only her obvious desire that you should leave, but my own knowledge of what you did to her in the past."

"What *I* did to *her*?" Kevin shouted. "Did she tell you how she started it? Did she tell you that she was screaming and throwing things? Did she tell you that she's just as guilty as I am?"

Kevin's anger was at a boiling point. He slid his hand slightly behind his back, underneath his pack, ready to pull out his gun, bracing his body for whatever came next.

"Quick," said Henry to Cindy. "Go find Jean and call 911. We'll deal with this."

Cindy nodded, running around the side of the tents to the pathway that led towards Jean's house. Kevin tracked her with his gaze and turned to follow, but Manis had circled around behind him to block his path. He swiveled his head from Manis to Henry, trying to decide which one to attack first.

25

Cindy ran as fast as she could, knowing Jean had a cellphone for emergencies. She wondered how Kevin had found her. The only explanation is that he had somehow dug the information out of Vanessa and she hoped her friend was okay.

When she got to Jean's, she bounded up the steps and banged on the door, desperately hoping that Jean was inside. With deep relief, she heard light footsteps approaching until it opened.

"My God, Cindy. What's happening?"

Cindy tried to calm her breathing. "The man who assaulted me and killed my little girl somehow found me here. We need to call 911."

Jean's heart sank. She had carefully guarded the privacy of Tamanass, not wanting her community on the radar of local authorities. In the 20 years since she founded the property, there were only two occasions when county sheriffs had visited them, both times responding to anonymous complaints of people who had heard about the ayahuasca use and reported it as illegal. Neither of those visits resulted in any real problems, just vague warnings. Even the deputies in this part of the country were inclined to respect people's privacy. Live and let live.

But now, as she looked at the panic in Cindy's eyes, there was no question about what to do.

"Of course!"

She quickly stepped to a desk drawer in her living room, extracted her cell phone, and punched in the numbers. She put it on speaker so that Cindy could listen.

"This is 911," said a dispatcher. "What's your emergency?"

"We have a violent trespasser on our property and need your assistance now!"

"What's your location?"

Jean had long ago learned that GPS coordinates were best for locating Tamanass, so she relayed them to the dispatcher.

"All right," came the response. "We'll dispatch a county deputy as soon as we can, but your remote location might take a while. Please keep your phone handy for updates. Meanwhile, are you and others able to stay out of danger?"

Jean looked at Cindy.

"Who is there with your ex?" she asked.

"Manis and Henry," she responded.

Jean felt a flash of relief, knowing the capable fierceness of Manis and suspecting the same from Henry. "We're doing what we can to contain the situation, but please hurry."

"We will," said the dispatcher. "One last question. Do you know the name of the trespasser?

"Kevin Rhodes," blurted Cindy, "birthdate June 3, 1982, and if you're able to check his name, he has a record of one, possibly more assaults in California."

"Thank you for that info," said the dispatcher. "Standby and keep your phone handy."

"We will," said Jean as the call disconnected.

"We have to go back and see what's happened," said Cindy.

"Yes, but carefully."

At the instant, a gunshot echoed over Tamanass, the sound as incongruous as a siren wailing in a library.

"No!" exclaimed Cindy.

The two of them raced out of the house, down the steps, and jogged towards the tent area. In the distance, they could see a small crowd gathering to witness the disturbance. With all the mass shootings in America, Jean felt Cindy's panic, afraid of a wider disaster. Even at an enlightened place like Tamanass, people were attracted to a fight. When they reached the circle of community members, Jean assumed her role as their leader.

"Let us by, let us by. Step aside."

When they got to the tents, neither of them found what they had expected. Kevin was seated on the platform that held Henry's tent, his pack on the ground, his hands tied behind his back. The gun was in the dirt nearby. Both Manis and Henry towered over him. Kevin's head was hung, his chin nearly touching his chest. He looked up at Cindy as she got nearer, and instead of defiance or rage in his eyes, she saw only defeat. He had no cuts or bruises from a violent fight, and neither Manis nor Henry seemed to be wounded.

"What happened here?" Jean asked.

Manis turned to look at her and Cindy, then his eyes scanned the other members of the community standing in a circle.

"We were just having a meaningful conversation with Kevin. Isn't that right, Henry?"

Henry was not as calm as Manis. Both his hands were clenched at his side, his shoulders rigid, his jaw set in a mask of anger. But Manis's words were like a soothing tonic and he slowly relaxed.

"Yeah," he said. "A conversation about taking responsibility. About what to do when everything in your life turns to shit and you need to decide whether you're going to live or die. I've become sort of an expert on the topic."

As he said those last words, Henry tightened his fists again and lifted them in a menacing gesture. Manis gently placed his hand on Henry's arms and coaxed them back down. All during this exchange, Kevin had continued to hang his head, but now he lifted his face and turned towards Cindy.

"I fucked up," he said. "I know I have to face whatever happens to me."

He turned his gaze back to the ground and seemed to choke for a second, struggling to find other words. Then he looked again at Cindy. "And I'm sorry for everything."

It was the most unexpected thing she had ever heard,

and Cindy was sure that her surprise showed on her face. "There's nothing you can say that will make things right. I just know I *never* want to see you again."

Jean reached over to Cindy and squeezed her arm. Cindy dug inside herself to find other words that followed the lead of what she had learned from Manis, from Tamanass, from the wider perspective imparted to her from Mother Ayahuasca. They came from a place that suddenly opened up inside her.

"I was violent also. Maybe I need to forgive myself before I ever deal with the memory of you."

There was a murmur from the gathered members of the community.

"We love you, Cindy," said someone.

A siren sounded in the distance, gradually growing closer. Manis approached Kevin. "Come with me."

Kevin stood up, averting his gaze from Henry and the others, but as he passed Cindy he lifted his eyes to hers. The expression in them was so lost, so beaten, that it carved its way into Cindy's consciousness and touched a small part of compassion she still held for her ex-husband. She simply nodded at him as Manis led him away.

The sheriff's deputy had arrived with knowledge of Kevin's assaults against both Cindy and Vanessa, the outstanding warrants discovered when the county office accessed an interstate database. He handcuffed Kevin, placed him behind the screen of his patrol car, then drove off.

During dinner, one community member after another expressed their love for Cindy with kind words and hugs. Henry marveled at the genuineness of it all, realizing again how long it had been since he had lived in the midst of a supportive family.

Later, he and Cindy were seated on the platform in front of his tent, the very spot where Kevin had slumped with his head hung and hands tied behind his back. It was a beautiful summer evening in the Pacific Northwest, twilight like a lullaby, and Henry recalled the sense of peace that had descended upon him in the forest sanctuary. He thought about how the cosmos flowed onwards in a never-ending stream of time, regardless of the drama that played out on this tiny vessel human beings called Earth. The conflict with Kevin was already receding, and he felt surprised at just how quickly he was able to start letting it go.

After her initial panic and anger with Kevin's appearance, Cindy had also found a surprising ability to recapture some calmness. She sensed that some part of her past had resolved itself, and that her understanding of it would unfold in the days ahead exactly as needed.

"What *really* happened with Kevin?" she asked.

Henry shook his head, as if in disbelief. "It was uncanny. I was ready to brawl, to dodge bullets, to tackle him and take him down. I was all in. This reservoir of anger, this fight or flight response of adrenaline I learned on the streets, made me want to tear into him for everything he did to you. I crouched and got ready to pounce."

Henry took a deep breath. "But Manis was quicker than I imagined. He feinted one way, drawing Kevin to one side, then sprung the opposite way, wrenching the gun from Kevin's hand and pushing him back on his heels. Then

Manis fired a shot into the sky. 'Hear that?' he said. 'That's the sound of the violence that will not only tear others apart, Kevin, but tear apart whatever is left of your soul.'"

Henry shook his head slowly. "Manis used that same tone as when he described his journey to the debriefing circle. Again, it was uncanny. How could he stay so composed? It was like music that calms the savage beast, in this case not only Kevin, but me as well."

"What did he say then?"

"I can't remember all of it. I was trying to quiet the rush of blood in my ears. But as it faded, I heard Manis describing how violence only leads to more violence. He talked about how there's always another way, another chance to choose a different path. Then, unbelievably, he even expressed his love for Kevin, telling him that he could, at that very moment, choose to change the trajectory of his life and start evolving into a higher form of humanity. That he could make a new start, no matter how dark things had gotten for him. It was the pure essence of what I have experienced here at Tamanass."

Tears began to run down Henry's cheeks. "Do you realize how surreal that whole scene was? I was sure that it was so weird and out of place that Kevin would just scoff and try to attack us again. But like I say, it had a calming effect that was almost eerie. I could see from Kevin's eyes that he was taking it all in. Like he needed it."

Henry wiped his face with his hand. "I think Manis knew he wasn't only speaking to Kevin, but to me as well. He somehow knows that the course of my life is changing, and I want to embrace a new future. He knows how I've resorted to violence too many times in my own life. Maybe it's because he had chosen a similar path with Antifa."

Cindy reached up to wipe the remaining tears from Henry's face.

"Anyway, the anger just seemed to seep out of Kevin's body. He wasn't even resistant when I got some rope from my tent and tied his hands behind his back."

"Manis is amazing," she said softly. "He was speaking not only to you and Kevin, but to me and every other person within earshot. He's a true teacher. What he's learned on his life journey is a gift to all of us. Who knows if Kevin really heard it. I'm skeptical, but I need to focus on my piece, not on him. Nothing will change what he did, but I know that harboring hatred doesn't return my child. It's strange. In a way, I think the vision I had was partially preparing me for this moment."

She sighed. "Anyway, for me, it's that kind of wisdom that I needed—that I still need—from this place. It's why I returned."

They lapsed into a comfortable silence, holding each other's hands as darkness descended and the stars appeared like a blazing triumph of mystery. After about an hour or so, Henry reached up to caress Cindy's cheek.

"You want company tonight, or would you rather be alone?"

She looked at him with an odd, searching expression. "After all that happened today, I need some time alone. I hope you understand."

"I absolutely understand. Sleep well."

"You, too."

Henry crawled into his tent, exhausted from the rollercoaster emotions of the day's events, and he soon fell into a deep slumber.

In her own tent, Cindy was wide awake. Images from her life played across her mental screen like old movie footage. She saw herself as a girl, always obedient to her parents, never wanting to cause friction. She recalled her years in school, pandering to her peers for acceptance. She thought of both families expecting that she and Kevin would marry, a script she felt too fearful or lazy to challenge. She replayed her time with Kevin, their passionless relationship like singles under the same roof. She winced as she remembered her avoidance of his gambling addiction, using work and denial as defenses. Finally, she thought about her pregnancy and the futile hope that a child might spark new intimacy in their marriage and make things whole.

Then she relived their fight. Her rage, throwing books and a lamp at him, screaming with a wrath she had suppressed for too long. She saw his face as he leaped across the room to attack her, an animal expression of complete abandonment to his own fury. Then the blows on her body, especially her womb.

The memory of that violence had been too intense to fully recall until this moment. It had just been fragments that caused her to cringe and turn away. But now, as she clearly felt what had happened, the truth of her life's arc became all too apparent. It was as if she had telescoped out to view her own timeline, and she knew that the violence inflicted on her from Kevin was a physical manifestation of the violence she had rained upon herself for so many years. She wasn't releasing Kevin from blame. Far from it! He had victimized both her and Sarah! But she also saw how she had denied her own power and uniqueness, letting family and society dictate too many of her choices.

She vowed again to seek greater freedom, to never again submit to the control of anyone or anything else. After the legal divorce from Kevin, which she was determined to get as soon as possible, there would be no man, no job, no institution, no ideology that would ever again usurp her sense of self. A meeting of equals was what she needed, each person powerful in their skin.

That turned her thoughts to Henry. She remembered what he had looked like when she and Jean had found him standing near Kevin. His fists were clenched, his face set in a mask of anger, his eyes full of venom. He claimed to have made great strides here at Tamanass, and she felt no anger or potential violence in his responses to her. Only gentleness, openness, and concern. But had the beast inside him really been tamed after only a few weeks? Was it a mistake to get involved with a man who might, even at some future date, make her relive the abuse she had experienced with Kevin? She didn't think he would harm her, but she also knew how wrong she had been about so many things over the course of her life.

With a longing for liberation, she finally drifted to sleep. In her dreams she found herself back in that clearing in the woods, leaning towards the child/woman named Sarah. But this time, she lifted her baby in her arms and the two of them began to dance around the arboreal sanctuary, the grass and needles soft on her feet, the vault of heaven above them like the jeweled landscape of an Arabian night. She felt herself alternate between laughter and tears until she became aware of another presence. She turned to the pathway that led into the clearing and saw Henry there, a gentle smile on his face.

She stopped her dance, holding Sarah tight against her chest protectively. She didn't know how to respond. Should she take a step towards this man who had so suddenly appeared in her life? This man who was still healing his own wounds. Would he be a fruitful addition to her new path or end up holding her back with dictates and expectations of his own? A part of her felt apprehensive at his sudden presence, and another part felt magnetically drawn towards him.

She stayed frozen in that moment of her dream as the two of them gazed at each other. She felt as if the conflicting emotions would tear her apart.

26

For the first time in years, Henry slept soundly, descending into depths rarely visited, like bathing in the Ganges. When he awoke, he had a lingering feeling that an important dream had just slipped out of reach along with its message, but he was content to feel the relaxation that suffused his body, mind, and soul.

He unzipped his tent and crawled out to the light of day, immediately turning toward Cindy's tent. It was gone. Nothing left but scuff marks in the sand that covered the platform.

What the hell? He knew that when he left her the previous night, she was processing the day's events. Had he missed the cues? Had she been more traumatized by Kevin's appearance than he realized? Had he failed her in some way?

Trying not to think the worst, he wondered if he might see her at breakfast and get an explanation. He made his way to the Ark, and even though the meal wouldn't be served for a half hour, there were people gathered around the tables sipping coffee and herbal teas. As he scanned the room, he noticed Jean against the far wall motioning to him with her hand, urging him to join her outside. He followed as they stepped into the crisp morning air and thin sunlight.

"Do you know where she went?" he immediately asked.

"Just come with me to my cabin."

He followed her at a brisk pace along the pathways, then mounted the steps to her front door and went with her inside.

"Have a seat," she said, motioning to one of the chairs surrounding a small table. "I have something for you."

He sat and watched as she went to her desk and picked up a small, folded piece of paper, returning to sit across from him at the table. The wrinkles around her eyes showed concern. She slid the note across to him. "I found this pinned to my door this morning. It was inside an envelope with your name on it."

He unfolded the note to find a simple message scrawled in neat handwriting: *Meet me on July 12th at dawn on the Golden Gate Bridge.*

That was it. Short, cryptic, not at all what Henry had expected from her. "I don't understand. When we said goodnight last night, she seemed calm enough. I never would have predicted this."

Jean nodded. "I wouldn't have predicted it either, but as I thought about it this morning, I realized I wasn't really surprised."

"What do you mean?"

"I've had a chance to observe Cindy on more occasions than you. Between her first visit to Tamanass and these last few days, I have had the impression that the wounds caused during the violence with Kevin, including the loss of Sarah, have drawn things to the surface that are deeper than any of us realize."

Henry nodded thoughtfully.

"I'm sure you've noticed how mercurial her moods can be," Jean continued. "I think those were signs that she's still wrestling with something profound, maybe even still running."

"Running from what?"

"From her own pain. From memories or realizations about her past that she hasn't fully shared with any of us. Or perhaps from the words spoken to her during the most recent ceremony. Or maybe she's running to something. I can't really say, Henry. I just know it must have to do with what Sarah told her in that vision."

"She shared those words with me," said Henry, "and I don't know if I should keep them confidential."

"I'm not asking you to tell me, but it might help clarify how you and I can respond to her in the most healing way. I think that's why she left the note on my door rather than your tent. She wanted both of us to decipher this together."

Henry looked at the note again, then into Jean's eyes, coming to a decision.

"She said that the image of Sarah as child, then woman, beckoned her to come closer. When they were close enough to touch, Sarah said, *Mother, child, listen to the wildness of your womb. Only you can decide your future.*"

Jean nodded, her eyes thoughtful, and remained silent for a full moment. Henry didn't interrupt her, still shocked by the morning's turn of events.

"This is what I feel," said Jean. "Whatever life-changing decisions Cindy feels she needs to make, it obviously includes you, Henry. But I know you've struggled with your own decisions about how to move on from your grief. If you decide to follow the request of this strange note, you could be opening yourself up to another world of hurt. Cindy may know exactly what she wants. Or she might remain unstable for a long time."

Henry took a deep breath. "Hurt has been the background of my life for so many years. And I've been anything but stable myself."

"I know, but I've sensed some healing in your short time at Tamanass. Am I right?"

"You are, but it's not just because of the hospitality extended by you and this community. It's not even the beauty of the sanctuary you shared so generously. It has been Cindy's entrance into my life. She has accepted me for who I am. She has drawn words and feelings out of me that long needed to be spoken. And her touch has been magical."

Henry thought of their lovemaking under the stars, followed by the almost supernatural peace that had descended upon him that night as she lay sleeping softly by his side.

"It sounds like you've already made your decision."

"I guess I have. I need to see this through, whatever

the outcome."

Jean reached across the table and took his hand in her warm grip.

"Then please know this. You are always welcome at Tamanass, Henry Thornwood. As you leave, go with a knowledge that there really is a spirit guiding you and protecting you on this exact path you are meant to walk."

As Henry heard those words that would have seemed so alien to him just a few weeks prior, they had the ring of truth.

"Thank you," he said, squeezing Jean's hand and looking deeply into her eyes. "I'm eternally grateful."

Henry packed up his things and said goodbye to a few people, some of them hugging him with more warmth than he expected given his short stay at the camp. Then he made his way down the wide pathway that led to the exit from Tamanass. As he neared the guard house, Manis emerged. He looked as refreshed and strong as ever, exuding stability and wisdom.

"Are you leaving us so soon, my friend?"

By way of answer, Henry passed him the note that Cindy had written.

Manis read it then looked up.

"Obviously from Cindy. I noticed her absence at breakfast."

"Yes. She packed up and left during the night."

Manis shook his head with a bemused smile. "That woman is stealthy. I didn't hear her pass and I rely on my senses to monitor every coming and going."

"Same with me. I didn't even hear her take down her tent."

Manis glanced at Henry's backpack.

"I can see you've decided to follow her."

Henry nodded, and Manis burst into the same laughter that erupted from him during the debriefing, a warm sound that echoed through the forest and enveloped Henry.

"Good man! You're following your guide. You're taking the risk to move into the next phase of your evolution. I know this is the truth!"

Henry felt buoyed by Manis's words, reaching out with both of his hands to clasp Manis's hands. They looked into each other's eyes in one of those moments that Henry knew he would never forget.

"Go in peace, brother," said Manis.

Manis watched Henry recede down the path that led to the highway. He was still amazed that Cindy had crept past his tiny home undetected during the night. He didn't blame her for feeling traumatized after Kevin's encroachment, and he chastised himself for allowing the man on the grounds. There could have been bloodshed, and the mere presence of a gun, the intent of violence, would ripple through their community for a while.

He had laughed and been encouraging of Henry's choice to accept Cindy's invitation. To him, following one's intuition was a sign of strength, something that had repeatedly proved true in his own life. During the standoff with Kevin, Manis had watched Henry soak in a different response to conflict. It was like a visible dismantling of his body armor, one that Manis understood well. He trusted that the man was on a path to broaden and deepen his life.

But once again, Cindy's sudden departure gave him pause. He could only hope that whatever message she had received during the recent ceremony would be healing and not lead to more instability.

He stretched his arms over his head and took a deep breath. Lately, he had begun to feel restless, as if his time at Tamanass was nearing an end. But for now, in the silence that followed Henry's parting, he simply said a version of a Navajo blessing for the two of them that he had learned among the Diné.

"With beauty above you may you walk. With beauty all around you may you walk."

27

Henry continued down the dirt road towards the highway. When he reached it, he set off at a brisk, determined pace, sticking his thumb out to see if any of the occasional vehicles would pick him up. It wasn't long before an old Chevy pickup swerved to the shoulder of the road. Henry jogged to the open passenger window and looked inside. A young, bearded man in a denim shirt smiled at him. He had pulled his long dark hair into a ponytail, and a silver earring shaped like a crescent moon studded his right ear.

"Throw your pack in the back," he said. "I'm going all the way to the city and you're welcome to come along."

"Perfect. I appreciate it."

Henry hoisted his gear into the truck bed, then clambered into the passenger seat. The truck smelled of old marijuana smoke, but Henry's impression was that the man wasn't stoned. Otherwise, he would have asked to be let out.

The man released his right hand from the steering wheel and extended it to Henry.

"My name's Jacob."

"I'm Henry."

"Good to meet you."

Jacob pulled the truck back onto the road. It was an older vehicle but the cab was immaculate. A small Native American totem hung on a silver chain from the rearview mirror.

"By any chance are you coming from Tamanass?" Jacob asked.

"As a matter of fact, I am. You've been there?"

"Just one time. They held a three-day retreat that featured some Indie musicians I follow from the city. That place has a cool vibe and it's legendary around these parts."

"Yeah," said Henry with a smile. "Cool is one word. Refreshing is another. Or maybe even enlightening."

"Were you living there?"

"Just for a short time, but I'm on my way to an appointment in San Francisco."

"Ah, the city by the bay," said Jacob. "Now there's a place that's having a huge number of problems, especially with the homeless. I guess once you make yourself a sanctuary city, you open the floodgates. I've heard it's gotten so bad that major corporations are abandoning their office buildings in the financial district."

Henry was quiet for a moment, carefully deciding how to respond. "Have you ever had a conversation with someone who was experiencing homelessness?"

Jacob stiffened a bit, wondering if Henry was being

confrontational.

"Not really. I've had a few friends who were couch surfers during hard times until they got back on their feet. But never a face-to-face with someone actually living on the street."

Henry immediately thought of Roger wearing his kente-cloth headband, bopping to tunes from his old iPod. He thought of the worn faces of men and women lined up to receive coffee in Freedom Camp. He thought of Aisha staring through the hospital window with concern about her little daughter, Tanika. Had that only been a short time ago? So much had happened since then that it seemed like a distant reality.

"I've lived on the street on-and-off for years," he said, "and when I get to San Francisco I will probably pitch my tent alongside those homeless you're mentioning."

"I didn't mean to be offensive. I just know there are a lot of problems in those tent cities. Drugs, human trafficking, and huge amounts of waste in the gutters."

"That's all true, a symptom of some of the worst of our social ills. But the challenge for me, and I guess for everyone on the planet, is to see the humanity in each person. My time at Tamanass deepened my awareness that we are all connected on fundamental levels that we don't recognize. We need each other. We just can't seem to acknowledge that truth in a way that changes us."

Henry sighed and looked at the broad Columbia River Gorge passing on his side of the truck. Timeless beauty, human struggles, always an interplay of the two, and a planet that was groaning under the weight. He thought of the imaginary game he and Cindy had played on the way to Tamanass.

"So, yes," he continued. "Homelessness in San Francisco or anywhere else is definitely a problem. But it's also an opportunity. You hear me?"

"I do," said Jacob, nodding his head. "We are the world."

Henry chuckled, letting his seriousness dissipate. "Something like that."

The two of them rode the rest of the way in comfortable silence.

"Where do you want me to drop you?" asked Jacob as they entered the city with its traffic and looming skyline.

"At the train station if you could. I'm going to take the Starlight Express."

"No problem."

Jacob knew the city well. He expertly navigated them to Union Station and pulled to the unloading curb. Henry quickly hopped out and retrieved his backpack, closing the door and then reaching through the open window to shake Jacob's hand.

"Thank you so much," he said. "I wish you all the best."

"Same to you," said Jacob. "And I thank you as well."

"For what?"

"For reminding me to look for the humanity in everyone I see. That was a gift, man. Peace out."

"Peace out," said Henry with a smile.

28

Henry used his debit card to purchase a window seat on the right side of the train, a chance to absorb the best views. The route would take him to Oakland, followed by a ferry ride to San Francisco, a total of 18 hours. He settled back in his seat and tried to be present to the beauty of the passing coastline.

Against that timeless panorama, he was struck by where his thoughts naturally flowed. Over the last few years, when he wasn't assisting others, it was his obsessive memories about Marsha that took center stage, dragging him into that nether zone between life and death, saturating him in the self-indulgency that had recently become so clear.

Now, with breathtaking views of the craggy Oregon coastline rolling slowly by the window, he was relieved that all he could think about was Cindy. The first time he had touched her, slathering medicated cream on her cut. The morning she had unzipped his tent to look in on him.

Making the rounds with her at Freedom Camp. Sitting on the overpass at twilight, sharing their life stories with a vulnerability he had not experienced in years. Their lighthearted banter as they took the bus along the Columbia River Gorge. Facing each other with naked frankness while showering, impish grins on their faces. Assisting other residents of the Tamanass community. The night of the ayahuasca ceremony and the otherworldly look on her face as she sat by the fire. The debriefing group and how she trusted him later to reveal the whole story. The turmoil surrounding Kevin's appearance.

But most all, the night they made love in the sanctuary clearing underneath the Milky Way. The unbridled release they had both felt and the look in her eyes as she looked down on him after their climaxes. Even then, was she contemplating her escape and the cryptic note she would leave for him?

He saw clearly what a risk it was to follow her invitation to the bridge. But he also knew with certainty why he had accepted it. Quite simply, he wanted her. He wanted to sit next to her, to hear her voice, to touch her, to let their lives intersect in every way possible. It was the beginning of a love that both thrilled him and scared him. And he knew that even if this strange rendezvous never materialized, he was grateful for the feelings she had stirred. He was thankful for the healing that had already taken place. It was not just the genesis of love, but the transition to a new will to live, to explore, to move on with his life.

What will this mean? he wondered. *Not just with her, but with my future? Can I ever go back to teaching?*

If not, maybe find an occupation born out of these years of wandering? How can I put all the pieces of these experiences into something that is meaningful for me and others?

The very fact that he was asking himself these questions brought a smile of anticipation to his face. He knew that whatever happened on the bridge at dawn, he would be reentering the world in a new and productive way. With the gentle hum of the train rolling beneath his feet, he fell asleep in his chair, awakening with a start as the overhead speaker announced their arrival in Oakland.

He grabbed his backpack and slung it over his shoulders, following a line of debarking passengers. The ferry station was in South San Francisco, quite a distance from the Golden Gate Bridge, so he bought a bus ticket to the Civic Center where he knew there was an established homeless encampment.

When he got there, he saw the colorful lines of tents pitched in rows, an orderly appearance that masked the presence of disorderly lives. The summer air, customary for this city by the bay, was cool, a soft breeze sweeping along the sidewalks. The morning fog had burned off, replaced by clouds that scudded overhead.

He strolled along the sidewalk, struck by how he felt at home in the midst of abject human poverty. Some of the residents were sitting outside their tents, others sealed inside them, others peering out through zippered openings as he walked past. One young man with a tie-dye headband lifted his hand in the universal peace sign. When he smiled, you could see that he was missing a host of teeth. Another woman had moved her sleeping bag and blankets outside the tent, lying prone on her back, arranging the covers so that only her face showed through the opening. She was snoring with a trust in her surroundings that amazed Henry.

Remembering that Roger might be in the city, he grew hopeful when he saw the flash of a kente-cloth headband on a Black man in the distance seated next to his tent. But as he got nearer, he saw with disappointment that it wasn't his friend.

The man noticed his interest. "Do you have a cigarette?" he called out.

Henry had purchased a few bottles of water and some granola bars at a bodega. "No, but I have a fresh bottle of water here. You want it?"

Henry pulled one from his pack and extended it. The man nodded and took it.

"Thanks, man. I appreciate it."

Henry nodded and continued walking. When he came to the end of the sidewalk, he sat on a bench near an old woman who was feeding pigeons with scraps of bread. The birds were strutting and cooing, competing with each other for every morsel.

"Where did you get the bread?" Henry asked as a way to strike up conversation.

The woman turned her face to him, and the first word that came to his mind was Methuselah. He had never seen a face with so many wrinkles, nor with eyes that seemed to radiate such wisdom. Another example, he thought, of the humanity residing in every denizen of the street.

The woman examined him closely, finally deciding that he seemed genuine, worthy of engaging in conversation.

"There's this bakery nearby and I scavenge the old scraps out of its dumpster in the alley. Some of it I save for myself. Some of it I share with the birds."

She threw another handful outwards, attracting even more pigeons. A few sparrows hung on the periphery, darting in occasionally to steal a crumb. Nature's pecking order.

"Do you know that St. Francis once preached a sermon to the birds?" asked the woman.

"I think I've heard that before, but I don't know the content."

"I can't recite all of it, but I do remember some of the words he supposedly said. 'God has given you the greatest of gifts, the freedom of the air. So please beware, my little sisters, of the sin of ingratitude, and always sing praises to God.'"

Henry smiled, treasuring the moment. Words from an old hymn rose in his mind, drawn from a childhood vault of the brief period when his family had attended a church.

"All things bright and beautiful," he said. "All creatures great and small, all things wise and wonderful, the Lord God made them all."

The woman laughed and flung another handful of breadcrumbs into the breeze.

"Exactly!"

She looked at him more closely, taking in his backpack he had placed at his feet.

"Did you just get here?"

"I did. I took the train down the coast from Oregon."

"Why San Francisco?"

"I'm supposed to meet someone at dawn tomorrow morning on the Golden Gate Bridge."

The woman's forehead scrunched. "That seems strange. Why so early and why the bridge?"

"I'm determined to find out."

She chuckled. "Must be a woman for you to travel all this way and make all this effort."

To his surprise, Henry felt himself blush.

"Ah, a lover," she said. "I knew it."

Henry laughed. "I can see that nothing gets by you."

"True, and it's been both a blessing and a curse."

Her face suddenly turned serious, the wrinkles deepening.

"If you have to be there by dawn, I wouldn't stay here at the Civic Center. You might not make it in time. You could climb down the embankment to the beach along Marine Drive just short of the bridge. If you go down around dusk, there are rocks along the cliff that you can sleep behind and no one will bother you. Just be ready because it'll be cold and foggy."

She wriggled her eyebrows. "Consider that some local wisdom."

"I appreciate it. You not only look out for the birds, but for strangers."

"Remember," she said. "Don't forget to show hospitality to strangers, for by so doing some people have shown hospitality to angels without knowing it."

Henry laughed. "I'm no angel, but you've been extremely hospitable. What's your name?"

"Samantha," she said, reaching out a hand covered

in a threadbare woolen glove.

"I'm Henry," he said, shaking her hand. "You have a beautiful soul, Samantha."

She dipped her head to acknowledge his compliment.

"All things wise and wonderful," she said.

It took him a while, but Henry found a pathway down the slope from Marine Drive to the beach below. Twilight was descending, and he could see the imposing outline of the great bridge in the distance. Just as Samantha had said, there were numerous boulders along the bottom of the cliff that provided shelter. He found an area of sand behind them, but instead of pitching his tent and making himself more visible from the roadway, he simply spread out his ground cloth and sleeping bag.

He broke out some granola bars and water as the last light of day grew dimmer. Along with it came the fog, reminding Henry of famous words from a Carl Sandburg poem, another one of the myriad quotes stored in his mental library: *The fog comes on little cat feet. It sits looking over harbor and city on silent haunches and then moves on.*

It grew much colder, so he donned his only warm clothes and crawled into his bag. Despite his earlier anxiety about the rendezvous in the morning, he felt only peace. He had a sense of satisfaction, not ego or pride, just an admiration for his own willingness to see something through to its conclusion. It was a strength that would inform and enrich the rest of his life. He wasn't just a starter or a quick sprinter; he was a finisher in the marathon of life, willing to go the distance wherever it took, even to death or new life. Seen in that light, he vowed to stop judging himself for how he had dealt with the grief over Marsha. He embraced it as a natural part of his temperament, a perseverance to see things unfold, come what may.

He shook his head in amazement, thinking how his life's path had led him from the lectern of a university classroom to a beach in the foggy dark, trailing the strange request of a woman whose motives were unclear. He sat up in his bag and faced the dark ocean swelling in the meager light of night.

"Here's to you, Cindy," he whispered in the dark, lifting his bottle of water in a toast. "Whatever your intent, I intend to find out."

He had charged his phone using a plug on the Amtrak train, so he set its alarm for 5:00 a.m. then laid back down in his bag. Whatever happened in the morning was meant to happen, and now all he could do was wait and trust in the goodness of the universe.

An ocean breeze, like a whisper of life, flowed across his cheeks.

29

San Francisco's summer fog engulfed the Golden Gate Bridge. It was near dawn, the appointed time, and already the mist was lightening from gray to a softer shade of white. Henry could hear early morning commuters streaming into the city on the opposite side, cloaked in gloom, their whooshing tires masking the roar of ocean breakers. Droplets of moisture clung to his dark hair and eyebrows.

As he walked along the bayside railing, he wondered if Cindy would be here. He recalled the warning he had received from Jean, and he shook his head. He was so far out of his comfort zone—led by his heart, not logic—that he barely recognized himself, a reminder that recent events had forever changed the course of his life.

He squinted through the dampness, rubbing his eyes, the density of the fog allowing only a few yards of visibility. He had been confident about his decision, but now he was beginning to feel foolish, even duped.

Suddenly, a figure materialized in front of him. A few steps further and he could see that it was her.

Her damp clothes clung to her skin, and she looked at him with those intense hazel eyes that always been so hard to read. She wiped a wet strand of hair from her forehead.

"I didn't know if you would come," she said.

"It seemed like the necessary thing to do," he said. "For both of us."

She nodded, gripped the railing, and began to lean her tall, athletic body forward, lifting both her feet off the bridge's sidewalk. He reached for her in a panic, his heart skipping a beat, and in that instant the fog cleared enough to glimpse the icy waters of the Pacific far below.

"What's wrong?" she asked. "Think I might go over the railing?"

"Why here?" he asked, trying to change the direction of her thoughts.

"Think about it, professor. I know you love metaphors. A bridge, a symbol of moving from one place to another. A way to make a transition. That's part of the reason. But also because it reminds me of a moment during my first trip up the coast to Tamanass. I stopped here, walked to this very spot, and wondered if the grief I was feeling would ever lift. I thought I might end the pain forever. That's something I know you understand."

Henry moved closer to her, but she shuffled back a few feet.

"They have a protective barrier now for people that jump," she said. "You might survive. Before it was there, do you know what would happen to a person?"

Henry was feeling more anxious now, wondering what she was up to.

"I read about it," she continued. "After a fall of four seconds, jumpers hit the water at around 75 mph. About 5% might survive the first impact, but then they would drown because of hypothermia in the icy water."

She pulled herself up again off her heels and leaned over the railing, her body extended even more this time, sending Henry's heart into his throat.

She eased herself back down again. "I even read about some famous jumpers. Like Roy Raymond, the founder of Victoria's Secret. He leaped from the bridge on August 26, 1993 and his body washed up in Marin Country. He was only 46 years old."

She laughed in a strained way, flipping back her damp hair. The beauty of her face shone in early light. "I did my homework. That's something I haven't always done in the past and I've paid for it. Have I done enough homework about you, Henry Thornwood?"

The fog around them moved in shifting sheets of gray, allowing momentary glimpses of the water below, then just as quickly enveloping them. The air was sharp with the smell of ocean brine. The sound of rush hour traffic from the opposite side of the bridge intensified.

Cindy raised herself up again to lean over the railing, this time even further.

"Please stop!" he said.

"What's wrong? Don't like the idea of someone leaning between life and death? Isn't that what you've been doing for so many years? Isn't that what you told me about

as we leaned back and forth on the bridge that first night we talked?"

"It's different now."

"Really? It's only been a short time. What's so different?"

"That was before I went to Tamanass. Before I met Manis and Jean, and all the others. But mostly, it was before I met you."

She moved back from the railing and turned to face him fully. "Tell me more. I need to know, because it's now or never."

He had no compunctions about sharing everything he was feeling. He had done the same with the first love of his life. He would do it now.

"You're right. I've been living in this limbo between life and death. I've been nursing my grief in a self-centered way. I didn't know if I would ever be able to start over again. I was dying by degrees, unwilling to do anything to end the process forever."

He dropped his hands to his side, palms outward.

"But my connection to you awakened me. I want to live. I want to see what the future holds. I want to see where our relationship will take us."

He let out a sharp breath, amazed at his vulnerability, as if he was again standing naked in front of her.

"And you traveled all the way here to tell me that?"

He shrugged his shoulders, then nodded.

She moved a couple steps towards him.

"Henry," she said, his name sounding sweet in his ears. "I never expected to meet you. God knows I never

expected it to happen in a homeless camp."

She moved even closer to him, reaching out to hold one of his hands.

"In all our conversations, in our serving others at Tamanass, and especially on the night we made love, I felt it also. I felt I could move forward. And I want it to be with you."

She took his other hand. "I now understand what Sarah was saying to me in my vision. Listening to my womb means listening to the wildest and deepest part of me, the part that will never again compromise my freedom. But it's also the part of me that wants to give and return love. It's a creative urge that may even lead to having another child in the future."

She looked keenly at him. "Does that scare you?"

"Not at all. But why did you have to tell me all this on a bridge at dawn?"

"Because I was still wary. Kevin's appearance at Tamanass reminded me of so many things. My whole life I've adjusted to fit into the expectations of other people. I prostituted my own freedom. I tolerated relationships and situations that didn't bring out the best in me. Could I trust my instinct, my womb, with another man? Could I trust you, Henry Thornwood?"

She squeezed both his hands tighter. "I figured that if you came all this way, you had to be serious about this thing that's happening between us. I needed to hear if you wanted to choose life, not this limbo both of us have been living in."

He gently pulled her closer. She didn't resist, and

they embraced each other firmly. He moved his lips to her ear.

"Right now, I have nothing to offer you but myself," he whispered. "But I know that both you and Tamanass have changed me. I'm ready to reenter life and society in a new way. I have a new confidence about my future."

"I only have myself to offer as well," she whispered in return. "And you know as well as I do that life is unpredictable. It promises nothing but today."

She hugged him even tighter.

"Then on this day, in this moment," he said, "and for as many todays as we might be given, I choose to travel them with you. I choose to love you with the best that is in me."

"Yes," she said. "This is the beginning of love. I feel it, too. And I want more of it."

She moved her lips to his and they kissed, a long, leisurely kiss that seemed to seal everything they were feeling. She then unfolded herself from him with a playful look in her eyes.

"Rock with me," she said, leaning over the railing. "Like that first night on the bridge."

They locked arms and leaned over the railing. Then back, then forward, then back. Cindy began to laugh, a contagious sound in the early morning, and he found himself laughing with her in a free and liberating joy. He looked down into the water of the bay below, letting the vertigo move through him, and he saw an early morning sailboat, a glint of sunlight turning its furled canvas a bright white.

"Let's do this, Cindy Rhodes."

"I'm with you, Professor Thornwood."

Without another word, they turned to walk back from the bridge into a new life. A seagull laughed from the suspension cables above.

Epilogue

Six Years Later

Through the windshield of their SUV, Henry and Cindy could see the overpass above Freedom Camp in the distance. It had risen again, even though the city had dispersed it numerous times, a testament to its tenacious residents.

"Those memories seem long ago," said Cindy, reaching over to put her hand affectionately on his thigh. "But also like yesterday."

"I know what you mean," said Henry, leaving his left hand on the steering wheel and placing his right one over hers with a loving squeeze. "I hope they're always part of any choices we make in the future."

From the back seat, their son, Alex, said, "Where are we going, Dad? Why did we have to get up so early?"

"You'll see. Just hold on."

Henry pulled into an area of gravel beneath the overpass. Arturo's car was already there, and he was leaning on the hood. He lifted his eyes and smiled as Henry, Cindy, and Alex got out of their vehicle.

Arturo and Henry hugged each other.

"I brought the thermoses and cups," said Arturo. "Also, something new, some simple breakfast sandwiches."

"Thanks, my friend."

"No problem," said Arturo. "After all, you're the Director of St. Francis. And I can't tell you how much pleasure it gives me to say that."

Arturo's eyes swung to Cindy. "How's my favorite realtor?"

"Business is booming," she said, "and our brokerage house has begun a political advocacy group for affordable housing in the city. We're making real progress."

Arturo looked down at Alex, placing his hand on the boy's shoulder.

"Hey, Alex. I'm glad you could join us this time."

"Well," said Henry, "as my old friend, Roger, used to say in this situation, let's get this party started.'"

Henry went to the front of the SUV, reached through the driver-side window and honked the horn, remembering how Roger had used his cowbell to summon the residents. Just like then, there was a response of rustling tents.

Arturo pulled out the thermoses, cups, and sandwiches from the back of his car. Henry put the box of sandwiches on the ground.

"Stand over here, Alex. After Arturo, your mother, and I pass out cups of coffee, you can hand a sandwich to each person. Sound good?"

"Okay, Dad. But what are we doing?"

Henry got down on his knees and looked lovingly

into Alex's eyes.

"We're making the rounds, son."

As he said those words, a deep well of gratitude filled his heart.

He kissed Alex on the forehead.

"We're making the rounds."

Acknowledgments

I would like to thank my wife, Donna, who has been supportive of my creative pursuits for so many years. Also, a shout out to Shawn and Jen Casselberry at Story Sanctum, for their editorial and design assistance. Finally, I am grateful for every person living in a difficult situation who has helped me understand more fully what it means to be human.

About the Author

Krin Van Tatenhove is a writer, visual artist, and spiritual adventurer. He was a Presbyterian pastor for 34 years, serving in a variety of settings but always an advocate for ministries of justice. He has also been an organizer for Habitat for Humanity, a substance abuse counsellor, a hospice chaplain, and director of a non-profit. His 40 years of professional writing experience have led to countless articles and 17 books. You can freely download most of his work—including art collaborations—by visiting krinvan.com. Krin holds a doctoral degree in ministry from McCormick Theological Seminary. He is married, has four children, and lives with his wife and disabled adult son in San Antonio, Texas.